NEW, IMPROVED MURDER

"Fast and funny, this first in a promised series bodes very well indeed. . . . As Dwyer delves into the advertising world, he meets Donna Harris, who is trying to start an industry newsletter. Dwyer first finds her 'endearingly wacky' and then falls in love with her, as will most readers. Ad-exec Gorman has a sharp eye and quick pen for people. After Dwyer and Harris team up with a couple of nifty closing lines, one looks forward to their next caper."

Publishers Weekly

"NEW, IMPROVED MURDER is potent stuff—a novel for anyone who looks for gritty realism in his crime fiction. Packed with incident, strong emotion, violence, wry observation, wit, and characters who linger in your memory. What more could you ask for? For my money, Edward Gorman is one of the best writers to come into the field in the past several years."

Bill Pronzini

"As fast-paced and attention-getting as a 30-second TV commercial."

The Washington Post Book World

Also by Edward Gorman
Published by Ballantine Books:

ROUGH CUT

NEW, IMPROVED MURDER

Edward Gorman

BALLANTINE BOOKS • NEW YORK

Library of Congress Catalog Card Number: 85-11838

ISBN 0-345-33378-0

This edition published by arrangement with St. Martin's Press

Manufactured in the United States of America

First Ballantine Books Edition: December 1986

To my son, Joe,
with admiration and love

ACKNOWLEDGMENT
I'd like to thank my editor, Brian DeFiore,
for doing me the inestimable favor of
saving me from myself.

IT WASN'T A PARK, REALLY, JUST A STRIP OF GRASS running along the river. In the summer it was a place for lovers, what with its picnic table and benches. Now, in November, with a steady, bitter wind slamming the gray water below into a jagged rock wall, it was home only for a few pigeons and stray dogs. Which was why the lovely blond woman in the tailored trenchcoat looked so out of place leaning against the rail above the river.

She showed no sign of recognition as I moved toward her, and I knew how bad a sign this was. Jane Branigan was almost neurotic about greeting you with deft little jokes and tiny, heartbreaking smiles. I should know. I lived with her for slightly longer than a year.

By the time I reached her, the noontime fog dampening my face, the chill deadening my fingers and knuckles, I saw that she held something in her left hand, something dangling just out of sight behind her coat. I shifted my steps slightly to the right to get a better look at what she was holding.

Jane Branigan held a .45 in her hand. Not the sort of thing you expected a woman who worked as a commercial artist, and who was the daughter of a prosperous trial lawyer, to have in her hand.

She didn't become aware of me until I was within three feet of her. Then she looked up and said, simply, "He's dead, Jack. He's dead."

From my years on the force it was easy enough to recognize that she was in shock. The patrician features, the almost eerie ice blue of the eyes were masklike. I was surprised that she even knew who I was.

"You'd better sit down," I said.

"Doesn't matter."

"Come on," I said. "It'll be better for you."

"He's dead."

"I'm sorry."

"The way he looked—"

My impression was that she was going to cry, which would have been better for her, but all she said was "Dead."

The .45 slipped from her fingers to the ground. I helped her to the park bench, sat her on the fog-slick surface. She was a statue, sitting there, poised, numbingly beautiful, as dead in her way as the man she mourned.

"Jane, can you hear me?"

Nothing.

"Jane, I have to ask you a few questions."

Nothing.

"Jane, where did you call me from?"

For now, anyway, it was no use.

I sat a moment longer staring at her, at her beauty that had turned my bed bitter and lonely, at her predicament, which rendered my old grudges selfish and embarrassing.

I sat there in silence, trying to think of what to say, what to do. Finally I had an idea. I touched her shoulder and said, "You remember the little puppy we almost bought that Christmas?"

Our first holiday together, shortly after we moved into our joint apartment, each of us in flight from the terrible first marriages. We'd gone to the city pound and nearly taken a small collie home with us. Then we'd decided, sensibly enough, that because both of us had careers, and because we lived in an apartment, such confinement would not be fair to the dog. Still, from time to time, I remembered the pup's face, his wet black nose and the pink open mouth as we wiggled our fingers at him.

Apparently Jane had a reasonably clear memory of the dog too. She didn't smile or say anything specific, but something like a response shaped in her eyes as she stared at me. I took her lifeless hand, held it, saw in the slight tightening of her mouth and the tiny wrinkles around her eyes the stamp of late-thirties on her otherwise flawless face. I felt a little sorry for both of us. Our lives had not been exemplary and we'd hurt many people needlessly along the way. It had taken her hurting me before I understood that.

Then I got up and went over to the .45. I bent down, took out my handkerchief, and lifted the piece as carefully as possible. It was unremarkable, the sort of weapon sporting goods stores sell as nothing more than a way to get you to come back and buy ammunition. I looked at it in my hand and imagined a prosecutor pointing to it dramatically in the course of a trial.

Then I went up to the phone booth on the edge of the hill and called 911. It didn't take them long to arrive. It never does.

2 EDELMAN, SHREWD MAN THAT HE IS, HAD LEARNED enough from the dispatcher to bring an ambulance along. Two white-uniformed attendants had helped Jane into the rear of the vehicle and taken her away. They would take her to the closest hospital and the police would decide what to do from there.

Edleman had also brought along a big red thermos full of steaming coffee, which we shared as we stood at the railing overlooking the river.

"You aren't getting any younger, Dwyer," he said, smiling, taking note of my gray-flecked hair.

"At least I've got enough hair to turn gray." I smiled back. Martin Edelman stands six-two, looks as if he trains at Dunkin Donuts, and is sweet enough in disposition to make an unlikely cop, a profession he took up only because, as he once drunkenly confessed to me, he'd been called a sissy during early years. Now the kids who called him names were pencil-pushers and Edleman had earned the right to ask them with his eyes: Who was a sissy and who was not? Like many of us, Edleman spends his older years trying to compensate for the pain of his younger ones.

We stood silently for a time, blowing into the paper cups

of coffee, watching a few straggling birds pumping against the dismal, sunless sky.

Then he said, "She's one of the most beautiful fucking women I've ever seen."

"Yeah."

"How do you know her?"

'She used to be a friend of mine."

"*Friend*. When we were growing up, *friend* usually meant somebody of the same sex, you know? I can't get used to the way that word is used today." He paused. "You mean you slept with her?"

"Yeah. We lived together for a year or so."

"This was after you left the force, I take it?"

"Uh-huh."

"You don't sound happy."

I stared out at the water. "I'm a little confused right now, Martin."

"The gun, you mean?"

"Confused about a lot of things. My feelings, mostly." He had been a good enough friend from my detective days that I didn't have much trouble talking to him. "I had all these plans for us, including marriage. She worked at an advertising agency and fell in love with a guy named Stephen Elliot there. She left me for him."

"A good Catholic boy like you should maybe think that God was paying you back for living in sin."

Both of us knew he was only half joking.

"It was more than shacking up, Martin. A lot more. I really loved her."

"This Elliot, that's who we're checking on now, right?"

"Right."

I had explained to Edelman that I'd had no idea where Jane had called me from when she'd hysterically begged me to meet her here by the river. But what with the gun and all her "he's dead" references, I thought that the police should check Stephen Elliot's house, which they were doing now.

"Heartbroken, huh?" Edelman said.

"Yeah."

"That happened to me, just before I met Shirley. This little Polish girl. Goddamn, she was cute. She kept telling me how much she liked me and I took her real serious. I asked her if she'd marry me and she looked like I'd asked her if she'd get down on the ground and push dog turds around with her nose."

"Well, then you know what I was like for a year or so."

"Greatest diet in the world," Edelman said. "I dropped thirty pounds. My parents wanted me to *stay* heartbroken."

I laughed. He was good company, a good man.

He took a sip of coffee, then said, "You think maybe you made a mistake leaving the force?"

"Sure. Sometimes I do."

"I mean, the acting thing—"

He paused, trying to be delicate. With my ex-wife, my mother and father, and every single person I knew on the force, what I want to do with my life will always be "the acting thing"—something pretty abstract and crazy, as that phrase implies.

What happened was this: One of the local TV stations asked me to play a cop in a public service announcement about drunk drivers. Easy enough, since that's what I was, a cop. Then a talent agent called and asked me if I would be interested in other parts on a moonlighting basis, which I was. A year later I'd appeared in more than two dozen commercials and was taking acting lessons from a fairly noteworthy former Broadway actor. Then my marriage started coming apart. I suppose I got obsessive about acting in front of a camera where I could put off the guilt and pain. I decided, against the advice of everybody I kenw and to the total befuddlement of my captain, to give up the force and try to become a full-time actor, supporting myself in the meantime with a P.I.'s license and employment with a grocery store security company, busting shoplifters and trying to figure out which employee's were stealing.

That was me, Jack Dwyer, thirty-seven, a man who'd

become a bit of a joke. Maybe more than a bit, as certain smirks and eye-smiles sometimes conveyed.

"It's what I want to do with my life," I said, and I could hear the defensive tone sneaking into my voice. If I'm so damned sure that what I'm doing makes sense, then why do I always feel the need to defend myself? Only my fourteen-year-old son seems to understand even a bit of my motivation. He always gives me a sad, loving kind of encouragement.

"Yeah, sure, hell," Edelman said, afraid he'd hurt my feelings. "I wanted to be a surgeon at one time."

I laughed. "Maybe you should start cutting people up. You know, practice it a while, see if you like it. The way I did with acting at first."

"You're a crazy sonofabitch, Dwyer. A genuinely weird guy."

But I couldn't keep up the patter any longer. "She's probably in big trouble."

"Probably. Yeah."

A uniformed man came running down the hill from his patrol car, through the slushy dead grass and the wraiths of fog and the winter cold.

"Malachie called from this Elliot's house," the patrolman told Edelman breathlessly. "Said there's a body there and that the building manager has positively identified it as Elliot."

Edelman shook his head and put his big hand on my shoulder. "Looks like we've got some problems, my friend."

3 "HE MUST'VE BEEN SOMEBODY," A DETECTIVE
named Dick Malachie said an hour later.

The *he* he had in mind had just been loaded onto a gurney and could now be distinguished only as a lumpy shape inside a shiny black bodybag. Two ambulance attendants, obviously bored with the scene, waited impatiently for Malachie to give the word.

"I count four different stations out there," Malachie said, parting the curtains. "And that's just the TV people." He offered the dozen or so people in the room—lab men, several lower-grade detectives, a doctor from the ME's office, and a lawyer from the County Attorney—something resembling a smile. "I hope wherever Mr. Eliot is at the moment, he appreciates the fact that everybody's making a big fuss over him." Malachie, a tall, slender man with dirty-gray hair and a beagle face, shrugged his shoulders and looked at me. "What did this guy do, anyway?"

"Advertising whiz."

"I guess I don't know what that means."

"He was creative director at an advertising agency. Before he got there, the place was almost out of business. He turned everything around."

"A hero."

"Sort of, I guess."

"The press must have known who he was." He nodded toward the street again. "The mayor getting shot wouldn't turn out this many people."

Edelman laughed. "The mayor getting shot would turn out twice as many. Give the people what they want and they'll show up every time."

Malachie, who wore Hush Puppies and a plastic pen-and-pencil holder in his shirt pocket, came over and tapped a ballpoint against the evidence bag that held the .45 Edelman had turned over to him.

The gun lay on a marble-topped gilt-wood center table worth many thousands of dollars. Over the past four years I'd worked several security gigs at antiques shows and had gotten to know something about their value. The table was indicative of the entire house—a modern Tudor tucked into a three-acre lot on the south edge of the city, just where the resort area began. It was a rich man's house, with several expensive Chagall prints on the walls and real Persian rugs on the floors. Outside were a BMW and a Porsche in the three-stall garage. I thought of the months Jane had lived here—a star-struck girl in the clutches of a legend.

"You knew the guy?" Malachie asked me, still prodding the .45 with the ballpoint.

"Knew of him."

"But you know the chick."

"Woman, I think you mean."

He looked up at me sharply, as if I had betrayed some bond between us.

"Oh, yeah, right," he said, "woman."

"I know her. Yes."

"She called you, Edelman said."

"Yes."

"What time was this?"

"Eleven-o-three. I looked at my watch."

"What did she say?"

"Not much of anything. She could barely talk."

"She must've said something."

"She just asked me to meet her in the park."

"When was the last time you'd talked to her?"

"Over a year ago."

"Kind of strange she'd call you, isn't it?" He wasn't being hostile. He just had a cop's curiosity.

"I suppose she remembered I'd been on the force."

"Edelman tells me you're an actor now."

"Sort of, I suppose."

"Kind of like that Eddie Egan in *The French Connection*, huh? He was a cop, too."

I smiled. "He's doing a little better than I am."

He shook his head. "Boy, I don't think that guy can act worth shit." Then he looked at me directly. "What did she tell you in the park?"

I told him exactly what she said, knowing that I was probably helping convict her. I told him about her "he's dead" statement and about the gun she'd held. I wondered if, subconsciously, I wasn't paying her back for the grief she'd caused me. But I doubted it. I had grown up believing in telling the truth, and that's how I'd conducted myself as a police officer. It wouldn't be like me to lie now. In most respects I was doomed to being a fucking boy scout.

When I was finished, I could see the case closing in his eyes.

He had the body not ten feet away, the murder weapon at hand, and his killer in a hospital within ten minutes' drive. He had an appreciation for my condition—he wasn't doing any macho numbers or acting delighted—but he was quietly happy that he would not have to go through all the tedium and disappointment of a murder investigation. Despite the way they are made to appear on TV, homicide cases are generally dull stuff.

From the front door a shocked male voice said, "I've got every goddamn right to be here. Now stand aside!"

I turned to see an elegant-looking man in a three-piece

blue suit that might have cost what I make in a year try to push past the uniformed officer at the door. The man was no more than five-nine and he was probably in his late fifties, early sixties, but his tanned, handsome face and his well-kept body gave him an intimidating presence.

I knew who the man was, of course. Bryce Hammond, the president of Hammond Advertising, where Jane worked, and where Stephen Elliot had been creative director.

Malachie, irritated that Hammond was being so pushy, started over to the man, angry already. I was a step ahead of him, walking over to Hammond and pushing out my hand. "Hello, Bryce, how are you?"

Hammond recognized me; we'd gotten along in a weird sort of way at all the office functions I'd gone to during my tenure with Jane. He just seemed shocked and a little confused that I was here.

"Jack—is Stephen—?"

I nodded. Then I pointed to the bodybag.

Hammond glanced at the plastic shaping itself to the dead corpse, then back at me. "But—" Nothing coherent came from his lips for at least another three minutes.

Malachie came up to introduce himself. I did most of the talking for Hammond, explaining who he was and why he was here. Hammond managed to say that he had called Elliot's home half an hour earlier, trying to find Stephen, when a policeman answered. The uniformed cop nodded that, yes, he had taken such a call.

Hammond looked back toward the gurney. "God, Jack, what the hell happened? Where's Jane?"

Malachie took that moment to nod toward the ambulance attendants. They looked eager, fighters waiting for the bell. They moved out immediately.

Malachie said, "Why don't you buy Mr. Hammond some coffee someplace, Jack?"

"Good idea," I said. I nodded to Bryce Hammond.

Malachie put out his hand and touched Hammond

respectfully on the elbow. "I'll call you tonight or tomorrow, Mr. Hammond. I need to ask you some questions about the lady involved and about Mr. Elliot's life lately."

"Of course. Yes. Certainly. Perfectly all right." Bryce Hammond was babbling in disbelief. He still hadn't gotten a handle on things.

"Now why don't you go with Jack here? All right?" Malachie said.

From across the room Edelman gave me a friendly wave and I waved back. There really were times I missed the force. For all the bullshit, there is a camaraderie that becomes a part of you. You don't find a lot of that in store security work or in auditions where thirty people are vying for the same part.

4

THE IRON SKILLET WAS NOT THE KIND OF PLACE Bryce Hammond was used to being in.

A hangout for the last dregs of the "Flower Power" movement, where the guys who work as day laborers and junkmen still wear their hair in ponytails, as if competing to see who can look as scuzzy as an R. Crumb illustration. The Skillet is nice for its total and utter lack of pretension, and for the abundance of home-cooked food you can get inexpensively. They've got real dark beer imported from Austria, and the battered booths are so steep you feel as if you've got your own private dining room.

"Eve of Destruction," which the management leaves on the jukebox as a goof, was ripping the air as we walked in. Bryce was as much a freak to the denizens as they were to him. They exchanged looks that were devoutly hostile.

I ordered coffee and a dark beer and, after a long minute of decision, Bryce did too.

After the waitress left, Bryce said, "Do you actually like it here?"

"Yeah."

"I'm surprised. You a former policeman and all." He'd had just enough time during our twenty-minute ride over to

13

compose himself, to face the reality of Stephen Elliot's death, and to start adjusting to it. He was himself again—at least enough to realize that a man of his stature did not belong here.

"Oh, I was in this play a couple of years back," I explained, "about some people in the antiwar movement and I came in here to study some of the folks. I ended up liking the place. Nobody tries to impress you and they almost never get into fights. You can play chess in the back and on weekends they've got some good live jazz."

He looked around. "Yes, but the people, their clothes—"

"They're laborers," I said, his attitude starting to irritate me. "They're not going to look like bankers."

He shot them a look of country club contempt, and then he turned his attention back to me.

"Is Jane—?"

I sighed, waited for our waitress to return. After she did I told him everything I knew.

"God," he said, "the poor kid. It really looks bad for her, doesn't it?"

I nodded.

"I'd better tell you what happened at the office yesterday." He pursed his lips again, his handsomeness no longer quite so attractive. "The police will find out anyhow."

I prepared myself for the worst.

"She stabbed him," he said.

I jerked in my seat. "Stabbed him?"

"Oh, just with an X-acto knife. But she stabbed him nonetheless. Right in the hand. There were several witnesses." He shook his head. "They'd split up three months ago, but she was still insanely jealous whenever she found out he was dating somebody." He sighed, stared at his hands. "I told him about office romances, how they could—" He looked up at me directly and evenly and said, "You know I'm ruined, don't you?" There was an edge in his voice that I knew could well be hysteria.

I made a pass at calming him down. "Bryce, things could work out. You don't—"

"Oh," he said gravely, "don't sit here and give me that bullshit. You know enough about advertising to know what I'm saying."

Thirty years ago Bryce Hammond had been the top copywriter and creative director in the city. Eventually he got so hot that he started his own place and prospered. But then, as always happens in the advertising business, his fortunes fell. Clients began to consider him too familiar, passé. He began losing accounts to the degree that he nearly went out of business. Then five years ago Stephen Elliot joined the Hammond agency, and almost immediately things turned around. The agency, thanks to many of Elliot's TV campaigns, was now back on top and hotter than ever.

That is, until today, when Elliot was murdered.

"Sonofabitch," he said. I didn't ask who or what he referred to. I just let him sit there with his anger and bitterness and anxiety and stare at his fists. After a while he said, "You think she did it?"

"I hope not."

"It looks pretty bad."

"Yeah, it does."

He shrugged. "Things turn around." He looked past me, at nothing, it seemed—at everything, his receding life. "I was nearly out of business once, as you well know. Nobody, not even my own accountant, thought I could turn things around. But I certainly did. I certainly did." He laughed. There was a lot of anger in the sound. "Or I should say Stephen did. He was the man of the hour, wasn't he?"

"That's what I've heard."

"A brand-new product, replacing the old one that had worn out." He tapped his chest miserably. "I was the old one."

The misery with which he said it made me aware that he was being serious, not just melodramatic. What an odd fate, to think of yourself as a product, just another box of soap.

"I don't know what the hell I'm going to do."

"Why not sit here and drink your beer?"

"I'm going to have to watch it crumble all over again. The whole fucking agency. Down the tubes. It won't happen overnight, of course. But in the next two years, one by one the important clients will leave me and—" He shrugged. "Fuck it. You're right, Jack. All I can do now is sit here and drink my beer. Unless this place serves something stronger."

"It doesn't."

"Somehow that doesn't come as a shock."

I got out my pocket-size notebook.

"What's that?"

"I want to ask you a few questions," I said.

"I thought you said I should sit here and drink my beer."

"Yes, and while you're doing that, I'm going to ask you a few questions."

He arched an eyebrow, then sank back in the booth. "You want my opinion?"

I sighed. "I think I can guess what you're going to say."

A kind of mourning touched his eyes. He looked older, tired. "I'm afraid I think she killed him. The police evidence is pretty overwhelming."

"Maybe it's all too pat."

His expression was more kind than patronizing. "Yes— maybe."

"Can I ask you a few questions?"

He smiled wearily. "Sure."

"I need to know the names of any close friends of Elliot's."

He smiled. "He was ambitious enough not to have any friends per se. He didn't have time for any; they were baggage to him. Besides, he might have to step on somebody, and he didn't want to feel guilty about it."

"You say he and Jane split up."

"Right."

"You know why?"

16

"Stephen didn't want to be tied down. That simple. He had looks, money, and he was the most selfish bastard I've ever known."

"You don't sound very fond of him."

He stared at me carefully. "Am I making myself a suspect? Don't answer that. Whether I am or not, I want to have my little say here. For all my faults, I'm a reasonably charitable man. I take a real interest in most people's problems and I try to help them out. There wasn't an ounce of that in Stephen, and for that reason alone I didn't like him."

"Any other reason you didn't like him?"

"You really are turning me into a suspect, aren't you?"

"I need to know the truth, Bryce."

He sighed. "Sure there were other reasons I didn't like him. For one thing, I was jealous."

"Why?"

"People saw me as pathetic. The agency bore my name, but everybody knew that he was really the main figure, not me. That's a kind of impotence. But I sure as hell didn't kill him."

"Well, if he didn't have any friends, can you think of anybody who might have wanted him dead? Besides Jane, I mean?"

"I thought about that on the way over here. I guess the first guy I should tell you about is an art director named David Baxter."

"Why would Baxter want him dead?"

"Baxter's wife was sleeping with Stephen. She works for me. Baxter found out about it a week ago. There was a very ugly scene in our parking lot."

"Can you give me Baxter's address?"

He did. "Anybody else?" I asked.

"This isn't a suspect, but it's somebody he hung out with. A media rep named Carla Travers, who sells time for Channel Six." He snorted. "Do you know about media reps?"

"I'm not sure what you mean."

"Some of them are the worst sort of people you'd ever want to meet—stupid, lazy and really treacherous. They make used car salesmen look like altar boys. They'll tell any kind of lie to make a sale." He smiled bitterly. "There's this little game they play. If the ratings say they're in last place, some of the sales managers just juggle the figures until they look good. It gets ludicrous—'we're number one,' but among midget Tasmanian transvestites, that kind of crap. Agencies are pretty well-connected against them because we have our own media buyers who know all about the false claims they make." Another head shake. "The people I really feel sorry for are the small retailers. The bad reps really feed on them."

"Aren't there any *good* media reps?"

"Oh, sure, of course. Some very good ones. Honest, professional, honorable, but . . ." He frowned. "But too many of them peddle gossip and lies instead of helpful information."

I smiled. "Other than that you're crazy about them."

"Yes," he said, smiling back, "other than that. Anyway, Carla Travers may be able to help you. She and Stephen had an odd kind of relationship."

"What's that mean?"

"I'm not sure, actually. I once saw him spit in her face—he didn't know I'd looked in a door by accident. But after that I saw them together several times at the Conquistador."

The bar he mentioned was the latest fashionable place for media people and the more successful actors.

"You were being literal, about spitting in her face?"

"Quite literal."

I glanced at my notebook again. "Anything else you can help me with?"

He shook his head. "No."

I stood up. "Why don't I give you a ride back to your car?"

Van Morrison thundered on the jukebox. He was probably my favorite singer. "Blue Money." I wanted to stay and listen and think nice things about my son and my future as an actor and remember what it had been like to hold Jane Branigan during the night when the lightning scared both of us and drew us closer together in a naked, silky, pagan embrace.

Suddenly I felt an urgency to be alone. I made a quick trip of taking Hammond back to his car.

5 SHE WAS WAITING FOR ME WHEN I GOT HOME——IN THE gloom of my parking lot. A chill wind was working up as I slammed my car door. Her headlights snapped on and her four-year-old Chevrolet started dogging my tracks as I walked to my apartment. She pulled up beside me.

"Hi," she said. In the gloom I could see that she was attractive. I could also see from the way her red hair touched the top of her car that she must be at least six feet. She wore a white turtleneck and a blue blazer. She was probably a few years younger than I.

"Hi," I said.

"You're Dwyer, aren't you?"

"That's me, okay."

"You cold?"

"Cold?"

"Yes. Cold. The weather, I mean."

Boy, was I enjoying myself. "Yeah. I am kind of cold, now that you mention it."

"Would you care to get in?"

"Your car?"

"Yes."

It was crazy enough to interest me, to divert me from reality. I shrugged, walked around the car, got in.

The first thing she said was, "I probably didn't do that right, did I?"

"I beg your pardon?"

"The way I talked to you and all. That probably wasn't the right way."

"Right way for what?"

"The right way to get a story."

I sighed. "You mind if I smoke?"

She smiled an affecting smile. For the first time I noticed that one of her eyes strayed just a tad, like Karen Black's. For some reason I find that not only cute but sexy.

She showed me her own pack. "You mind if *I* smoke?"

We lit up.

"Over there all right?"

"Over there?" I asked.

"To park."

"Sure. Over there looks like a swell place to park."

She drove maybe six feet into a parking space that faced a retaining wall. Nice spot. In the rearview mirror I could see the dying pink of the dusk sky.

"I probably have to get better at this, don't I?"

"Oh, I don't know," I said, "I don't really see all that much room for improvement."

"I mean just saying 'hi.' It doesn't sound official."

"Sounded pretty official to me."

"Really?"

I looked at her. Frowned. "Do you mind telling me what the hell we're talking about?"

"See? You didn't think I was worth a damn, did you?"

"Maybe you did a wonderful job. But first of all, before I can judge that, I need to know what the hell you were *trying* to do."

"I was trying to come on like a reporter."

"Oh. Yeah. Right."

God, it was all nutsy.

"You ever watch 'Lou Grant'?"

"Yeah," I said.

"It was my favorite TV show. Especially Linda Kelsey. She was really good."

"Yes, she was."

"Anyway, after I got fired, that's the idea I had. To be a reporter."

There was something tirelessly and endearingly wacky about her. At other times I would have felt properly swayed. Now all I could feel was sorry for both of us. This woman, fetching as she was, belonged in a home of some kind.

"Why don't we start with the basics?" I said.

"Like what?"

"Your name."

She laughed. "See, that's how nervous I am. I forgot to tell you my name."

"You still haven't."

She lauged again. "See, as soon as I saw you, I got so nervous I forgot everything I was going to say. I just started gibbering. That's a word my mother always uses. Gibbering."

"Do me a favor, all right?"

She shrugged. There was a neurotic quality in the shrug, though I couldn't exactly tell you what I mean. "Shut up."

"What?"

"Let's just sit here and smoke our cigarettes. I've OD'd on talking for now."

"But I haven't told you my name yet."

I turned on the radio and put my head back and closed my eyes and took the smoke deep into my lungs and held it there. She was tuned to a Top 40 station that was playing a Michael Jackson song. I felt perfectly safe. She was nuts, but she was harmless. With my eyes shut, I became aware of her perfume. It was a gentle scent, sweet. It fit her.

After awhile she cleared her throat. She said, "My name's Donna Harris and I'm the publisher and editor of a newsletter called *Ad World*."

I opened my eyes. She sounded much more together now, and as soon as she mentioned being associated with an advertising publication, I began to understand why she was here.

"I have nothing to tell you," I said.

"Are you angry?"

I just stared at her.

"I didn't mean to make you mad." She frowned. "See, dammit, there I go. I can't really be assertive when I need to be."

I didn't say anything this time either. She had another go at it. "Maybe Jane Branigan didn't kill Stephen Elliot."

I must have looked curious about her remark.

"I've been doing a story on Elliot for my newsletter. I had an appointment with him this afternoon at his house. When I got there I saw the police and I started asking questions. One of the policemen was real helpful. He mentioned you and he mentioned Jane. I just looked you up in the phone book."

I'd make a lousy spy. I left too many easy trails for people.

"I'm not an expert on advertising," I said, "but I don't think I've ever heard of your newsletter before."

"Oh," she said, as if I were the world's leading dope. "The first issue hasn't been published yet. That's why this is such a break for me."

For the first time she touched me. Literally, I mean. She put out a hand and placed it on my shoulder.

"I'm sorry, I didn't mean it that coldly. I just meant—"

I sighed. "I know what you meant."

"Just that—"

"Just that Stephen Elliot being killed will make a big story for your inaugural issue."

"Yes. Exactly." She paused. "Especially if I can help solve the murder, scoop everybody else."

So that was it.

I sat there in the darkness, listening to her heater bang

away at the chill, watching a perfectly lovely woman prove herself over and over again certifiable.

"How long have you been a journalist?" I decided to have some mean fun with her. Right now it was the only game going.

"Why do you ask?"

"Curious."

"Well, not real long, I admit."

"How long?"

"Oh, roughly two weeks, more or less."

"More or less."

She hurried on. "But I've done a lot of writing. Copywriting."

"I see."

"I've won a Clio and probably fifteen Addys."

I smiled, liking her despite myself. "You get fired?"

In a very tiny voice, she said, "Yes."

"So you decided to start a newsletter?"

She nodded.

"Being a journalist isn't easy."

"Neither is finding another advertising job. I've really been trying hard. After the agency I was with lost their biggest account forty-one ad people were dumped on the market—including me." She shrugged again. Neurotically. "I've either got to make this newsletter thing go or—I've only got five months' worth of money saved up. At most."

"Something will come along."

"You don't think much of the newsletter idea, huh?"

"Not really."

"I figured it out. If I can sell four hundred subscriptions throughout the state at fifty dollars a year, I can easily pay the printing bills and have a decent salary left over."

My father used to have notions like that. A lot of schemes that the whole family found sweet but hopeless.

"You going to work on it?" she asked.

"The case?"

"Yes."

"I suppose."

"You don't think she did it?"

I looked at her. "I hope not."

"Maybe we could work together."

"I don't think so. Sorry."

"Maybe I could be helpful."

I rolled down the window several cracks. The heater was getting to me. "You're very nice," I said. "You really are. And I hope you find a job soon."

"Shit," she said.

"What?"

"Oh, nothing." There were tears in her voice. "When I was married that's how my husband treated me. Every idea I had was 'charming' to him. Which translated to the fact that I was crazy. I admit I get carried away sometimes but—"

She must have heard herself. Her panic, there in her four-year-old Chevrolet.

I reached over and patted her hand, and for just a moment I wanted to keep touching her. She had a wonderful hand.

I got out, then put my head back inside. "I wish you luck. I really do."

"You still in love with her?"

Her question rattled me. I tried to think of an appropriate answer. Maybe the real answer was one I didn't want to admit. Then I said, "I don't know."

"She's very beautiful."

"Yes."

"Maybe after all this is over you can get back together with her."

"Yes. Maybe."

"Well," she said.

I closed the door, walked away.

A DAY LATER I MET JANE'S PARENTS IN THE LOBBY OF the hospital where, despite what the police told the press to the contrary, their daughter was being held prisoner.

Mrs. Branigan had never liked me. A matron who had started life on a farm upstate and who had eventually become the wife of a successful trial lawyer, she used her good fortune as a kind of judgment about others. Anybody who had not done as well as she and her husband were ultimately to be found lacking. Some longstanding moral curse, perhaps.

Mrs. Branigan wore a tweed coat cut to hide the abundant flesh of her middle age. She had more luck with makeup, which almost took the hard edge off her otherwise handsome face. She held her sixty years with an imperious regard, like a weapon.

Her husband was her twin, a ruddy, white-haired man whose girth in his vested suit and whose melodramatic style suggested both alcoholism and a minor case of megalomania. He had once told me during a holiday visit to the family manse—it was not quite a mansion, but it didn't miss by much—that he had once been a Catholic, but was now a

Presbyterian because he'd gotten tired of the joshing at his country club. I've always admired people of deep conviction.

When I first saw them I got the distinct impression that they might be plotting to hire an assassin. Rage burned in their faces and gave them a nervousness that was almost ugly. When they saw me their rage only deepened. Here was the man their daughter had not only lived in sin with— the lower-class man who'd been previously married—but worse, whom she'd *wasted time with*. At one point in our relationship her parents had tried to bribe her away from me by offering her a free and extended trip to Europe. She'd been thirty-four years old at the time.

I wasn't sure why I went in there. Maybe there's some real masochistic compulsion in me. More likely it was because, on my way up to see if the police would let me see Jane, I wanted to know if the Branigans had learned anything new.

I didn't offer my hand. I knew better. I wasn't that much of a masochist. Instead, I said, "I don't think she did it."

"How reassuring," Mrs. Branigan said tartly.

Branigan had the grace to look embarrassed. "I'd forgotten. You were a cop once, weren't you?"

I nodded.

"Have they told you anything?"

"Nothing since yesterday," I said.

"She didn't do it." He said it absolutely.

"No. I don't believe she did."

Mrs. Branigan said, "You hadn't been seeing her again, had you?"

"Don't trouble yourself," I said. "We really had broken off, Mrs. Branigan. I hadn't put my filthy hands on her in over a year."

Mrs. Branigan looked as if my language made her physically ill.

Mr. Branigan slammed a big fist into an open palm. "My

God, I can't believe this. This just isn't possible." He started pacing.

Mrs. Branigan watched him. I watched Mrs. Branigan. She said to me, "The police have said that she called you."

I tried to take some of the anger out of my voice. "Yes, Mrs. Branigan, she did."

"I want to know why."

"I suppose because I used to be a policeman. I suppose she thought I could help her."

Now Mrs. Branigan softened her tone. Even some of the contempt went out of her eyes. "Well, as a former policeman, what do you think?"

"Do I think she's guilty?"

"Yes."

"No."

Mr. Branigan said, "He was a real bastard. She was calling us nearly every night all the time he was breaking things off with her. He went out of his way to make the end as unpleasant as possible."

"He even—he even brought another woman to their apartment one night when he thought Jane had to work late," Mrs. Branigan said. There were tears in her eyes. "I suppose I have to say that much for you—you treated her well."

"There's something you never quite seemed to understand, Mrs. Branigan," I said. "Jane broke up with me—not the other way around. She convinced herself I was this really terrible guy so that she could justify going off to live with Stephen Elliot. I know that's not a particularly noble thing to say at a time like this, but I think we should set the record straight."

Mr. Branigan pushed out his hand. He looked as if he might consider shaking hands with me, then put his hand away quickly.

"Did you get a chance to talk to her?"

"Not much," I told him. I sketched in our meeting in the park.

"Then she didn't mention the older woman in the museum?"

"No."

"She followed him one night. He went to this museum. He spent several hours there with a much older woman."

"Do you think that has some bearing on what happened?"

"I don't know."

"Did she say anything else about the woman? What museum it was, for instance?"

Mrs. Branigan spoke up. "Only that there was a traveling Van Gogh show."

"Over the next week," Mr. Branigan said, "he met with this woman several times. In a restaurant there was a scene between them. The woman slapped him."

Elliot seemed to have had a predilection for scenes. Spitting in Carla Travers's face. Getting slapped in a restaurant by an older woman.

"When Jane asked Elliot who the woman was he got very upset and told her to never mention the woman again—if she wanted to live."

"He actually threatened her, physically threatened her life," Mrs. Branigan said. Her voice had started to keen again. For the first time in my life I found myself feeling something resembling warmth for her. At least a bit.

I put my hand out and touched her shoulder. She surprised me by not jerking away. "I'm going to do all I can to help her."

She looked at me. It would be nice to say that she offered me a warm embrace and told me how wrong she'd been about me and that I was a wonderful guy.

But all she said was, "We would appreciate that, Jack. Very much."

But that was something. She had never called me "Jack" before. Somehow she'd managed to talk to me without every using my name.

"Yes," Mr. Branigan said, "yes, we certainly would

appreciate it. Very much. We'll be staying at the Hilton if you need to get in touch."

I nodded and went upstairs on the elevator.

The uniformed cop listened to my story patiently, walked down the hall with squeaky shoes, and called his superior. He came back shaking his head.

They weren't going to let me see her.

7 HE HAD ARTHRITIC HANDS AND WASTED EYES, AND IF he had much more to live on than his social security, I would be surprised. He came in once a month and tried, as he was trying tonight, to steal a five-pound tin of ham. He was a lousy shoplifter. I was literally afraid that he was going to work himself into such a terrified state—the way he looked around, the half hour he took to get the ham up to his overcoat pocket—that one of these nights he was going to fall over from sheer fright.

I watched him for five minutes, then walked to the back of the discount store where I was pulling a security gig this week. I had gone there after leaving the hospital, hoping the evening would provide me with some professionals and a few games of cat and mouse. I needed the adrenaline of clean, cold pursuit. Busting old folks didn't qualify.

I placed my sixth call of the evening to the number listed as belonging to "C. Travers" in the phone book. If Bryce Hammond was right, the lady could give me all sorts of useful information about Stephen Elliot, including why he'd spit in her face one day.

There was no answer. Again. Either she was a busy

woman or she had disconnected her phone. I'd been trying to reach her since the day before.

On the floor, I watched the old man again. He had started into his head-swerving phase, looking around for store dicks like myself.

Satisfied that he was not being observed, he wrapped a gnarled hand around the ham and began to push it into his pocket. I moved quickly, afraid he might be observed from the manager's office.

"Hey," I said.

A look of mortification and pure horror filled his face. I touched his hand, guided the ham back to its place in the display.

"You sure that's the ham you want?"

His eyes were ancient, watery. His bones were hard, but his clasp was soft.

"Huh?" he said, yelling loud as a deaf man.

"I think you picked up that ham by mistake, didn't you?"

He stared at me a long moment, then started getting tears in his eyes. "Yes, I guess I did. By mistake."

I could imagine him savoring the ham—sliced and served warm in sandwiches. If the poor bastard had enough to afford bread.

"Fuck," I said.

"Huh?"

"I said fuck?"

"Fuck what?"

"Fuck everything, old man."

I picked up the ham and a loaf of white bread—I wasn't doing him any favors—and laid them in his arms. Then I took a ten-dollar bill from my pocket and put it into his.

"What're you doing?"

He still sounded scared.

"You won the store lottery."

"What say?"

"You won the fucking lottery," I said.

He looked confused.

"Just take the ten and go up front and pay for this stuff, old man."

"Huh? I never heard of no store lottery."

"Sure. Now hurry along, okay?"

"Goddamnedest thing ever happened to me."

I would have just given him the ham, but all security people have to take lie-detector tests and my largess at the store's expense would have shown up.

I pushed him along, walking behind him to the aisle split, which took me back to the phone and C. Travers. Nothing.

The apartment I lived in smelled of steam heat. In bed I ate an apple and read through a script I would be auditioning for the next day, this one having me as a garage mechanic dedicated to only one thing, your gosh-darn satisfaction. You betcha.

I slept very well, awoke around dawn, luxuriating in the feel of my body against the sheets, which were warm in some places, cold in others. I lay there for a time and thought of crazy Donna Harris. She made me feel good— her innocent and somewhat misplaced aggressiveness.

After a shave and a shower I got in my Datsun and drove over to Carla Travers's place.

She lived in one of those new condominiums along the river, steep and secret in firs and pines.

A few sleepy-eyed people were escaping from her section. They looked at me—even though I wore a new tweed jacket, button-down shirt, and pressed chino pants— as if I had been dropped off here by a muggers' touring bus.

In the lobby I found her name, pressed her button, and went up before she could say anything into the speaker. There wasn't a security door in the place.

Her hallway was golden with sunlight patterned through the firs. This was going to be a beautiful morning, not the kind you expected in gray November.

I put a hand on her doorknob at the same time.

The knob turned easily in my hand.

Three minutes later, after no response, I knocked again.

After a total of ten minutes I twisted the knob to the right and went inside.

The apartment was wide and expensive and nicely furnished with contemporary and colorful graphics on the wall, but, curiously, it lacked a personality.

I said, "Hello," but I realized it was only a formality. I closed the door behind me and went in.

Three rooms later I learned that she liked to cook in a wok—she had three of them—had expensive and florid taste in clothes, was sentimental about huge stuffed animals, and had a record collection that ran to Neil Diamond and Barry Manilow.

The final room I checked seemed to be a kind of den, a small room that a family would have used as a bedroom. In it she'd put a single bookcase and filled it with a lot of pop-psych and you-can-win type books, a small desk with air bubbles in the varnish that indicated she'd probably finished it herself, a straight-backed chair, and a file cabinet that promised to be the most interesting thing in her entire apartment, especially considering that on top of the cabinet was a framed photograph of herself and Stephen Elliot, arm in arm, at what appeared to be a resort.

For the first time since Jane's arrest I had a feeling that I might actually be making some progress.

I knelt down, my knees cracking as I did so, and started to pull the top drawer from the cabinet, when I heard something behind me creak.

Whoever it was moved accurately, crossing the distance between the closet where he or she had been concealed and bringing whatever it was right across the back of my head.

Before I slipped into darkness I had time to realize that my instructor at the police academy would be very ashamed of me for being so careless.

8 WHEN I CAME TO THE FIRST THING I DID WAS OPEN my eyes slowly and begin to feel the back of my head. The pain was a steady throb, which, if I remembered my first aid right, was a good sign.

By the time I started to roll over on my side and to think about getting to my feet a female voice, part nicotine and part liquor, said, "I didn't mean to hit you so hard, but you probably had it coming anyway."

She had pulled out the straight-backed desk chair and sat on it rather mannishly, a peroxide blonde with a Kewpie-doll face made even cheekier by bad drinking habits. She had long ago sailed past forty and a lot of makeup and garish clothes were trying to deny the reality of her fifties.

"You tried to get in last night, didn't you?"

"No."

"Don't bullshit me, friend."

"I didn't. You can believe it or not." I held the back of my head and prepared myself to stand up. It was going to hurt.

"Don't move. Not till I tell you."

I sighed. Laid my head back down. Carefully. Maybe she was doing me a favor after all.

"You know about me, don't you?"

"I assume you're Carla Travers, if that's what you mean."

"Boy, you're a regular goddamn comedian, aren't you? You trying to say you don't know about Stephen Elliot and me?" The heat and slur of her words told me she was drunk.

"That you were lovers, you mean?"

"Yeah, lovers, that's it," she said sarcastically. "Lovers."

"I know two things about you and Elliot. One being that you had your picture taken together at some resort and the other that one time he spit in your face."

"That wasn't the only time, you can bet your buns on that." Then she paused. "Say, you really don't know anything about us, do you?"

"No, I don't, as a matter of fact."

"Then what the hell are you doing here?"

"I came to talk to you."

"Right. You tried to bust in here last night."

"Can I stand up?"

"Yeah. But move very slowly and no funny stuff."

When I finally got to my feet, when I finally got a look at her, I saw a woman trapped in the high comic style of the local beauty parlor. There was enough brass in her demeanor to bounce quarters off. "She sent you, didn't she?"

"She?"

"Jesus, how long you going to keep this up?"

I could see what Bryce Hammond had meant about media reps. Real charmers. Here was a bowling queen and stevedore rolled into one, and got up in a kind of sexy pink grandmother slacks-and-blouse set.

For the first time I saw that she had a silver-plated pistol in her hand. Probably it was more decoration than anything else, but in a room this small it would do the trick.

"So you didn't break in here last night, and you don't know about me and Stephen, and you claim that she didn't send you."

She was making my head hurt even worse, handing me three different mysteries to solve, not one of which I could even guess at.

I started getting wobbly and worked my way over to the couch and sat down. Gently.

"I'm a private detective," I said.

She frowned. "For real?"

"For real."

"You gotta be working for her then?"

"Who's 'her'?"

She chose not to answer my question. "You tell me who hired you."

"Nobody hired me. I volunteered."

"Wait a minute, your name wouldn't be Dwyer, would it?"

"Yes."

"You're Jane Branigan's old boyfriend."

I nodded.

"That bitch." A look of real misery came into the doll-blue eyes. "She killed Stephen. That bitch."

"I don't think she did."

She started to talk, but a cigarette hack got her halfway through the first syllable. Clutching her gun, her fleshy body began doing a grotesque kind of cancer dance right there on the chair as the cough got worse.

"Shit," she said as she concluded.

"At least," I said.

She glared at me. "It isn't funny."

I shrugged. "I suppose it isn't."

"So why'd you come here?"

"I thought maybe you could help me prove that Jane is innocent."

"Listen, all the grief that spoiled rich bitch gave Stephen, I wouldn't help you no matter what."

"She didn't kill him."

"That isn't what the police think."

"Police make mistakes."

"Not in this case."

We took a minute to rest and then we went back at it. I started. "Whatever you think of her, she can be a nice woman under the right circumstances."

"Christ Almighty," she said, a malignant gleam in her eye, "your gonads are still in an uproar over her, aren't they?"

I could feel myself flush, but more at her delicate use of English than her insight.

"Hell, no wonder you want me to help you."

I didn't wait. "Why did Elliot spit in your face that night?"

She was angry. "None of your business."

"If I call the police they'll make it their business."

"You go ahead and call the cops if you want. I'll just tell them how you tried to break in here last night."

We took another rest. Then, "Tell me about Elliot."

"He was a classy guy." She gave me an odd look, one I couldn't read at all. "At some things."

"At creating ads. He was the best, according to everybody in the city."

She smirked. "I guess maybe you've got more faith in people's judgment than I do."

I was still trying to put her implications together—what the hell was she hinting at?—when the phone on the desk rang.

She stared at it for a time, as if she didn't know quite what it was.

"You want me to answer it?" I said.

"You just sit there and keep your goddamned mouth shut."

The phone continued to ring. Six, seven, eight, nine times.

Finally she picked it up.

I could hear a voice buzzing against the receiver. Carla Travers said nothing. Only listened. Then she said, "You know what I want and I better goddamn get it." With that she slammed the phone.

"Now can we talk about Elliot?"

She sighed. "You're kind of a pain in the ass, anybody ever tell you that?"

"No more than three, four thousand people a week."

"Yeah. I'll bet that's true, too."

"So what about Elliot?"

"He was a good little boy."

"Care to elaborate on that?"

"He had all these young women chasing after him—your girl friend was one of them—but that isn't what he was really interested in."

"What was he really interested in?"

She paused, opened one of the desk drawers, and pulled out a new pint of Seagram's. With a thumbnail, she expertly slit the paper banding the neck. "I don't suppose this is very ladylike," she said. She took a sailor's swig of the stuff, flinched as if she'd been shot in some vital place, and then closed the bottle and put it back in the drawer.

I could see her letting the stuff take effect, the way a junkie lets the smack flow all the way to the Amazon before moving, her eyes getting dreamy, her nerves steadier. If she lived long enough she'd wind up in a detox clinic.

She said, "I told him about my abortion one night when we were over here drinking and having a good time, and you know what he did?"

"What?"

"He cried. He took my hand and he held it and he cried right along with me."

I didn't know what to say.

"This was back in the early fifties, when I had my abortion, I mean. I even told him about the night it happened. Over a tavern. This medical student. The song 'Wheel of Fortune' kept coming up through the floor from below, and the sounds of the TV set above the bar. Goddamn 'Life of Riley' was on. I was cryin' and this bloody thing was bein' ripped out of me, and all I could hear was this laughtrack for 'Life of Riley,' all these people pretending to laugh. The kid with the knife screwed me up but good. I never could have kids again so I didn't see any reason to get married. I started selling TV time and that's what I've been doing ever since." She shook her head. "One of the boys, that's what happened to me. You remember the 'Dick Van Dyke Show'? That gal named Rose Marie? That's how I always thought of myself. One of the goddamned boys, whether I liked it or not."

She fingered the silver pistol in her lap. "Anyway, I told Stephen about my abortion, and he cried. He said it hurt him too."

This was the guy who had stolen my woman. Sympathy from such a creep was impossible for me to imagine.

"Of course, he changed when your girl came along. She was the first young one he ever got serious about." She patted with surprising delicacy at her cotton-candy hair. "He spit in my face because of your girl friend. I told him I wanted him to stop seeing her, that she was messing up the friendship him and me had."

"Did he stop?"

Nastily, she said, "She dumped you, didn't she?"

"Yeah."

"Well, that doesn't sound like he stopped, does it?"

"No, I guess it doesn't."

By now I could see that she was drowsy even though it was early morning. She said she'd been up all night. With her pistol and her Seagram's, no doubt.

"Earlier you said *she* sent me. Who's *she*?"

She laughed. "I had to find out for myself. You have to find out for yourself."

"Thanks for the help."

"Maybe it wouldn't even be healthy for you to know."

"Or maybe it would help me prove that Jane didn't kill Elliot."

She touched a hand wearily to her head. "At least I know it wasn't you who broke in here last night."

"Who was it?"

"Somebody who finally figured a few things out."

"Maybe you should call the police."

She glared at me with tiny, boozy, ugly eyes. "Yeah, I'm in some goddamn position to call in the frigging police, all right." She waved a drunken hand in the direction of the door. "Why don't you get out of here before you really start giving me a pain in the buns?"

I stood up, holding the back of my head every inch of the way. "You need help, Carla."

"I can handle it."

"Elliot's dead. He couldn't handle it."

"He was a little boy. He couldn't handle it, but I can."

I stared at her. She looked up, and for a moment we didn't dislike each other quite as much as we had for the past fifteen minutes.

"You really sound like you could use some help, Carla."

She smiled sadly. "Yeah. But then, I've been needing help most of my life and never got it, so why start now?"

I left her there, slipping out before the full weight of her bleakness and chaos could overwhelm me.

9 DONNA HARRIS WAS SITTING IN HER CAR OUTSIDE MY apartment house when I got back.

I pulled in behind her, got out, and strolled up to her car as if I were about to issue a ticket.

For all that my head hurt, for all that I was still trying to figure out Carla Travers's confusing story—and who, exactly, she had been talking to on the phone—I felt happier than I should have about Donna Harris being here.

In the daylight I saw that her redheaded beauty was more delicate than I'd first noticed—slight features and eyes that looked as if they expected pain at any moment.

She saw me touching the back of my head. "Boy, what happened?"

"Somebody hit me."

"You're kidding!" In her world people didn't go around hitting people. I wanted to live in her world.

"Unfortunately not."

"Who hit you? Boy, are you all right?"

"Boy," I said, "I'm all right. And boy, I'm not going to tell you who hit me."

"I guess I do kinda say *boy* a lot, don't I?"

"Boy, you do."

She smiled her lopsided smile. The warmth of it helped considerably.

"Maybe I've found out some things you should know about."

"Like what?"

"Feel like having breakfast?"

"No, but some black coffee sounds great."

"Get in."

The hardwood floor of the Iron Skillet was dappled with sunlight, like a Rembrandt painting, as we found a booth.

Donna Harris ordered pancakes, eggs, and bacon. Her six feet showed not an ounce of fat. She was one of those, eat all she wanted and metabolize it off.

"I found out something about you."

"Oh, yeah?"

"You're an actor."

"Sort of."

"No, a friend of mine who works in a talent agency downtown says he's seen your stuff. Says you're very good."

"Tell him to send me some work."

"You like it?"

"Yeah. Whenever I can get work."

"Boy, that's neat. Acting, I mean."

"Boy, it is."

She laughed. "I'm starting again, aren't I?"

I smiled. "I should tell you something."

"What?"

"I've had a tough couple of days and it's nice to see you."

"It's nice to see you too. I thought about you a lot."

"Probably because you didn't have anything else to do."

"You want a compliment, don't you?"

"I could use one about now."

She smiled. "People in hell want ice water, Dwyer."

While the waitress brought out food I watched Donna Harris get ready to eat. She did everything except rub her hands together. She was very different from the nervous woman I'd first met the other night. I liked her self-confidence now.

She managed to put food in her mouth, chew it, and talk all at the same time, and still look fetching.

"I've really been checking into Elliot's background," she said.

"And?"

"And he doesn't seem to have one."

"I'm not tracking."

"I keep asking people where he worked before and they don't seem to know. Apparently he showed up in the city several years back, bought himself the mansion on the edge of the city, and proceeded to become a fixture of the ad world here."

"Where did he work previously?"

"That's just it. Nobody seems to know."

I thought about that a minute. "What about the funeral home? What do they know about it?"

She snapped her fingers. "Boy, I should've thought about that." She smiled at me. "You were a cop once, right?"

"Right."

"No wonder."

While she did unspeakable things to the rest of her food I went in the back and called the funeral home where I knew the body was being handled.

The man I spoke with had a very masculine, articulate voice and was pleasant in what seemed a genuine way. I explained that I was trying to find some things out about the dead man and wondered if could help me.

"That's the curious thing," he said.

"What?"

"The other day I received a cashier's check for five thousand dollars and instructions that I should arrange everything."

"Nothing else in the note?"

"No."

"Have any relatives contacted you?"

"None. I've asked everybody who visited the body. They're all from local advertising agencies."

"Do you happen to remember what bank the check was drawn on?"

"First Federal, I believe."

"Well, thank you."

"Of course."

When I got back to the booth the big, beautiful, animal part of Donna Harris was wiping her face with the satisfied aplomb of a small child.

"Wow," she said, "that was great."

I told her what I'd found out and then said, "So how about you checking First Federal? Give them your journalist story."

She eyed me levelly. "There was kind of a smile in your voice when you said 'journalist.'"

"I'm glad you're not paranoid."

"You really think I can make it as a journalist?"

"I would think that anybody who could put food away the way you do is capable of anything."

"Very funny." Pause. "Do I eat like a pig, or what?"

She was getting self-conscious again, her self-confidence waning. "Can I ask you something?"

"Sure."

"The other day you said you weren't going to work with me. How come you changed your mind?"

"Now you're fishing for compliments."

"No. I'm just curious. Really."

"You want me to tell you that I found you fascinating and couldn't get you out of my mind."

"That would be nice, but that really isn't what I'm after. I just want to know why you changed your mind."

I smiled. "Because I like you. Because it'll be a good excuse to see you again. Is that better?"

"Much better." She sipped coffee. "Say, why don't you go to the bank with me?"

"I've got to do something."

"What?"

"Gee, I'm glad you're not a busybody."

"Sorry. That's a tendency of mine. I tend to be curious about everything—and very jealous."

"Fair warning, I guess, huh?"

"So what're you going to do?"

"I have an audition."

She started—surprised and apparently delighted. "Really? What's the part?"

"An auto mechanic."

"Boy, that sounds great."

"It pays scale and it'll be a good credit. But I probably won't get it."

"Why not?"

"I average about one part out of every eight or nine I go up for."

"You'll get it, Dwyer. I can feel it."

"In your bones?"

"In my bones, in my stomach, everywhere."

As a prognosticator, she left a bit to be desired.

10

JUST THE WAY HE LOOKED AT ME, I KNEW I wasn't going to get the part.

I was sitting in a straight-backed chair in a rehearsal hall along with maybe fifteen other actors of roughly my own age when the guy from the agency came in and started sizing us up.

You could tell he was from the agency by the way everybody from the production company started acting servile and making little jokes.

The way he eyed me and then dismissed me—like that—brought up familiar anger in me.

I can't explain to you what happens to me when I act, and even by trying to explain I have to hand in my macho badge. But it's something like—freedom. I have all this rage inside me, disappointment in myself, disappointment in the world, and somehow acting gets rid of it, at least for the length of time I'm performing.

I'm decent-looking enough, I suppose—six foot, slender, sandy, gray-flecked hair, features that are handsome without being pretty—and no doubt I'd like to reap some of the movie star rewards, the cars, the bank accounts, the famous friends.

But that isn't why I act. The relief from the rage, that's why. The closest approximation I can give you is running five miles on a hot day. Exhaustion has a way of dissipating anger too.

Of course, during the time I'd been thinking all this the agency guy was working his way down the line. He didn't look impressed by any of us. He stood there in his suede car coat and amber turtleneck, his hands shoved into his designer jeans, and frowned the way a child does when an animal fouls the living-room rug.

"Jerk off," I muttered.

Instantly several heads twisted my way. The other actors. They'd heard me.

So, judging by his look, had the agency man.

The man from the production company, trying to redeem the moment, threw his arm around the agency guy's shoulder and led him away, the agency man glaring at me all the while. I glared back. The bastard hadn't even let us read for the part.

"You got balls." The actor next to me laughed as we all stood up.

"Yeah," I said, "and they're worth about twenty-five cents each."

The media crowd, at least in this city, is fickle. An "in" place one month is an "out" place the next. Before making restaurant loans, bankers should first consult media people and see if a given loan is a good idea.

This month the place was called the Conquistador, and for all its dark wood and Spanish leather and burnished bronze instruments hung on the walls, it was the essence of modern urban tackiness. The waiters were got up as buccaneers, the waitresses as serving wenches. The serving crew was a bunch of college kids. They were getting their degrees so they could sit in places like these and have equally shameless college kids wait on them.

The bartender, a cordial enough man who looked as if he

probably threw refrigerators around for relaxation, had no qualms about pointing out David Baxter when I asked if he was there, which his answering service had told me he was.

Baxter and a fetching, dark-haired lady were sitting at a table in the darkest corner they'd been able to find. Baxter, at least from here, bore a resemblance fo Paul McCartney, that kind of snotty, preppie self-confidence. He wore a Harris tweed sport coat and a button-down white shirt, and held a pipe the way men do in fancy whiskey ads. He was pretty spiffy until I got closer and took a better look at his eyes. David Baxter had been crying, and quite recently.

His companion would have made Audrey Hepburn jealous, her graceful face and huge grave eyes a masterpiece of beauty and irony, the mouth suggesting laughter, the fixed blue eyes fatalistic. She wore a woolen jumper, the kind college girls used to wear, and a dazzling white blouse that enhanced the blackness of her hair. By the time I got to their table I saw that she, too, had been crying.

There were no words between them, just that terrible silence I'd gotten to know in my last days with Jane. . . .

They were deep enough into their grief that they didn't notice me. By now I had no doubt that I was looking at Mrs. David Baxter, the woman who'd been sleeping with Stephen Elliot.

I tried to make it as official as a private investigator's license can. I said "Excuse me" and pushed my open wallet in front of them.

They reacted as if they'd been drugged, slowly, without a breath of spontaneity. They stared at my license as if it were something new and unimaginable. Finally he said, "Yes?"

"My name's Dwyer. I'm a private investigator."

"Yes?"

"I would like to speak to you. To both of you."

He looked at her. She looked at him. There was a third chair at the table, empty. I decided not to wait for an answer. I sat down, signaled for a waitress, ordered a Heineken.

Softly, Mrs. Baxter said, "I don't understand."

"Why I'm here, you mean?"

She nodded. Again the sense that she was drugged.

"I'm trying to prove that Jane Branigan didn't kill Stephen Elliot."

She looked confused. "Oh, but she did. It's in the paper. I even saw it on television. She did kill him." Then she said, "Wait a minute. You're Jack Dwyer. You used to live with her, didn't you?"

"Yes."

For some reason my admission served to charge Baxter out of his stupor.

"Why are you here bothering us?"

"Just for the reason I told you. I'm trying to help Jane."

"Well, you certainly aren't helping either of us. We're—" For just a moment the anger gave way to the grief. I saw his hand tremble and I had the uncomfortable feeling he was going to burst into tears. "We're—" His eyes sought hers, but she was already removing herself from the table.

"I need to go to the rest room," she said, gone before anybody could complain.

He glared at me. "Thanks a lot." His preppie face was even redder close up. He looked like a very, very sad kid.

"I'm really sorry," I said. "I know what you're going through. I really do."

"Jesus," he said, "aren't you something? Do you moonlight as a shrink when you can't get work as a private investigator?"

I decided to hit him with it directly. "There's a good possibility you killed Elliot. I know all about the incident in the parking lot. He was sleeping with your wife."

He fought through his pain to his first real clarity. "Don't think it hadn't occurred to me, to kill him. Don't think it hadn't. But it just so happens I didn't, okay, pal?"

"Can you prove where you were the morning he was killed?"

"No. Can you?"

He was coming out of it. Given the sneer in his voice, I wasn't sure I was glad.

"How about your wife?"

He shook his razor-cut hair. "Did she kill him, you mean?"

"Yes."

He laughed. It was a high, ghoulish sound, odd enough to cause several nearby patrons to look over.

"You don't know a hell of a lot about Stephen Elliot, do you?"

"You're right. I'm beginning to think I don't." I thought of Carla Travers, at least ten years Elliot's senior, and their strange relationship.

"He was an aesthete, pal, he wasn't just some ass-bandit. And you don't kill aesthetes, you worship them." He was back into his funk again. He had hit himself with rage and feelings of inadequacy so long he was getting punchy, the way prizefighters get. And this, apparently, was the theme, this was what his wife had told him about Elliot, that he wasn't a mere lover, somebody who snared flesh, but a very special person. That's how Jane had once described him to me. "A very special person." Cliché that it is, it's not a phrase I'm apt to forget. Ever.

"Maybe she killed him without planning it, in anger."

The smirk was back. "No, pal, I'm afraid your little honey committed the crime all by her lonesome." He held his hand over his nose and tried to sniff up his sinuses after his recent tears. Then he sighed. "You know, it would be easier to take if my wife had killed him." He nodded toward the rest room. Bitterness had replaced rage. "This way he gets to keep her, even from beyond the grave, as the saying goes. She'll never know if he would have dumped her the way he dumped all the others. She'll prefer to think he wouldn't have—so he'll always hang on to her, even though I'm married to her."

"Then you're not going to get a divorce."

His admission surprised me. "I love her too much. Over the past three months, when it was all going on, I realized that I didn't give a shit about anything but her." He smiled dazedly. "You're married to somebody fourteen years, you tend to forget how important they are to you. Man, this was some goddamn reminder, believe me." He sounded hopeful and despairing at the same time, glad he had her back at least physically, terrified he could never reclaim her emotionally. He put out a hand. "Sorry I was such a prick."

We shook.

"Just the last few months—" He paused. "Well, you know how it goes."

When she came back her lips were bright red and there was a faint sparkle in her eyes. She sat down with a nice girlish primness, one appropriate to her jumper, and offered each of us a tiny smile, the way she might have placed a cupcake before us. "The tension level seems down considerably from when I left."

"It is," her husband said.

She turned to me. "You don't really doubt that Jane killed him, do you?"

"Yes, I do doubt it."

"I was—" She glanced at her husband, as if for permission.

He nodded. "Go ahead, Lucy. It's all right." He looked as if wasn't quite sure it was, but he was willing to find out.

"I was there when she would come up to his apartment and pound on the door," Lucy Baxter said. "She was like a wild woman. She'd literally fling herself against the door. She had to be hurting herself.

I had seen her like that, her despair turning into an animal frenzy that ultimately hurt her more than anybody. I wanted to help her, wondered if I could, wondered if, in fact, she wasn't guilty. . . .

"She was obsessive about Stephen—it didn't have anything to do with real love," Lucy Baxter said. "Why, she even threatened me several times at work. In front of other people." She shook her head. The tears started suddenly. "But she had no right to—to—"

She put her head on the table. A kind of moaning came from her.

Baxter moved over and put his arms around her. I wanted to ask her about the older woman the Branigans had told me about, but I saw that now was not the time.

Baxter slipped his arm around her, began to rock her, not giving a damn that he had an audience.

"We really need to sit here alone," he said.

I couldn't disagree with that. There was nobody else in the world who could deal with what had happened to them. I wasn't sure even they could.

I left there already planning ahead for how I'd spend my evening. Maybe I'd learn something important, or maybe I'd end up spending some time in jail.

11

THE REST OF THE AFTERNOON I DID ALL THE THINGS I've never learned to enjoy—shopping for groceries, picking up dry cleaning, paying bills. In the past two days I'd collected my paycheck from the security company and three different residual checks from commercials I'd done over the past two years. After subtracting my bimonthly child support payment, I didn't have a hell of a lot of fun money left over.

Up on First Avenue there's a tavern where local theater people hang out. Until ten years ago there was a dinner theater next to the tavern. That building is now one of those dead zones, where a new structure is constantly announced but never seems to get built. Theater people still use the bar, though. Indeed.

November bleakness was back by the time I rolled my Datsun into the parking lot. On top of a supermarket across the street the lights on a big Christmas tree popped on. I thought of my son when he was little, his delight in the season. Then I started thinking what a lousy father I'd been. Maybe that is what I really like about acting. It allows me to be somebody else.

The tavern was dark except for the glow of the jukebox

and the glow of the backlights that illuminated several rows of liquor bottles along the glass wall behind the cash register. A bumper pool game dominated the middle of the small floor space, dividing the booths on either side.

I wasn't four steps inside before I saw the guy I was looking for, a huge, red-bearded descendant of the Vikings named Rolfe Steenman. Days, he sold men's clothes in an expensive department store in the loop. Nights, he did what the rest of us did—picked up whatever parts he could find in plays, commercials, anything. His biggest distinction to date was that he'd worked on several of the spots that had made Stephen Elliot famous. I didn't really know Steenman, but I'd heard that he'd become reasonably tight with Elliot, and I thought maybe he could help me.

He sat at the bar, staring at his drink. A cigarette in the glass ashtray in front of him curled smoke into his face. He didn't seem to notice.

"Rolfe."

He raised his head lazily. He saw me, recognized me, and seemed to know instantly why I was there.

"Dwyer. How are you?"

"Mind if I sit down?"

"Free country."

I ordered a Heineken.

His size and his strength—he could easily have been an NFL fullback—surprised you in an actor. He was without grace, but he compensated for it with a powerful presence. He was also very good at comedy, which is what he'd done for Stephen Elliot.

"I suppose you know about Elliot," I said.

"Yeah. Your ex-old lady killed him." He didn't even make a pass at being civil.

"First of all, she was never my wife. Second of all, I don't think she's guilty."

"Oh, yeah. I forgot you were a cop once, weren't you?"

"I need to ask you some questions about Elliot."

He looked at me as if he were trying to decide how he

wanted to attack me—with his fists or his feet. "Jesus, man, I'm bummed out. Can't you see?"

The bartender came over with my beer. I thanked him.

I decided to push my luck. "When you were hanging around with Elliot did you ever know anything about him and an older woman?"

He smiled nastily. "You and every other fucking gossip-monger in this town. The 'older woman' happens to be his aunt."

I thought of how the Branigans had described this woman, how she had slapped Elliot when they'd been in an art gallery. That didn't sound like an aunt.

"You know anybody who'd want to kill Elliot?"

He surprised me by smiling. "I've got to give you your nerve, Dwyer. I told you I didn't want to talk about Elliot and here you are—still asking me questions."

He turned away from me, back to his drink. The bartender sensed that trouble might be coming. He had started to paw his apron nervously.

What the hell. I wasn't doing anything this afternoon, may as well get my face pounded in. "You know anybody who'd want to kill him?"

Without looking at me, he said, "A lot of people wanted to kill him."

When he spoke in a cool but not unfriendly voice the bartender looked relieved as hell.

Steenman turned to me and said, "A lot of people wanted to kill him. Maybe not literally, but figuratively. Because they were jealous. Here was this creative genius, this guy who could do anything, and they couldn't stand his talent or success. So they wished him the worst. Just like your girl friend, Dwyer. That's why she killed him. She couldn't stand the thought that other women might share a part of him. Just couldn't stand it." He was big and he was angry, but now he sounded more sad than anything. "The guy gave me a break, Dwyer. You know that? He saw something in me, some talent, that I didn't even know I had, and I'll always be grateful. He was a creative genius, yet he made room for people like you and me in his life."

I thought of how Lucy Baxter had spoken of Elliot—in the same kind of reverent terms, in the way you'd speak of an especially holy priest, a shaman.

"What about this aunt you mentioned?"

He shrugged. "I never actually met her, but he talked about her quite a bit. Even showed me a picture of her. His parents had died when he was young. She'd raised him."

"You know her name?"

"Angela. But I don't know her last name." He sighed. "He let me be a part of his world. It was exciting for me, believe me. He really knew how to live."

"Where'd he get all his money?"

"Hell, he had the top advertising job in the city."

"His house had an easy hundred thousand dollars' worth of antiques. The police are probably looking into his assets now. I suspect they're going to find a lot. You can't make that kind of money in advertising, no matter how successful you are."

But he hadn't heard me. He was just thinking of his gratitude to a man who'd taken him along, sort of a Gabby Hayes at the orgy. All the fancy parties, the fancy women, the heady sense of being loved and being envied. For a guy who looked like a Viking, it must have been something truly memorable.

"You sure you can't think of his aunt's name?"

"Uh-uh. And anyway, what's the big deal? She's just his aunt."

I stood up. Put down a bill for my beer. Stared at him a moment. He was genuinely sad. No doubt about it. He probably felt the same way about Elliot I had about John Kennedy; all Camelots come to an end.

"See you," I said, and left.

YOU CAN FIND DONNA HARRIS'S ADDRESS merely by looking in the phone book, which is what I did.

I drove over to the modern and modest brick apartment house, went to her mailbox-speaker, and announced myself.

"Boy, you really like surprising people, don't you?"

"Can I come up?"

"I don't look so hot and neither does my apartment."

"That's all right."

I knew I should have called, but all of a sudden I had this real need to see her.

The buzzer sounded in the small lobby and I went on up.

Donna wore a blue T-shirt with the state university logo on it and designer jeans. I could see she wasn't wearing a bra. I ached to touch her.

Her apartment looked as frazzled as she had the first night I'd met her. There was something endearingly sloppy about the paperbacks piled everywhere and the empty TV dinner trays that almost looked like decorator items and an occasional stray piece of clothing. The oblivion express apparently ran through here regularly.

"Now you know," she said.

"Now I know what?"

"What a shitty housekeeper I am."

"Gee, I don't think I'm going to hate you for it."

"My husband did. It was one of the reasons he divorced me."

"What were the other reasons?"

"Nosy bastard, aren't you?"

"I seem to remember you asking me a personal question the other night."

"He divorced me for several reasons, but the big one was that he fell in love with the court stenographer."

"You lost me."

"He's a lawyer."

"I see."

"And there was a court stenographer who was really quite beautiful and he fell in love with her. I don't suppose he could help himself, the rotten sonofabitch."

"I can tell you don't hold anything against him."

"Not a damn thing as far as I know."

We both stood there laughing. She got the sense of what was about to happen at approximately the same time I did. Only she moved away from it, stopped it from happening.

She took me on a nervous tour of the place rather than face what had happened between us.

Not much to see, actually: three rooms decorated with posters of people who had been fashionable in the seventies—everybody from Dr. Wayne Dyer to Jerry Brown—but who were now just voices from the media grave.

The kitchen was big enough to take rumba lessons in, but that was about all. The sink was piled high with dishes left in a drainer. On the counter were two boxes of doughnuts and an angel food cake. How did this woman stay so slim?

That was where it happened, where I reached out and touched her and brought her to me.

I couldn't remember having a kiss like that since high school. My head felt as if it were going to come off. I felt her tender breasts against my chest and the sway of her shapely hips against mine.

Then she pushed me away. "This is not what I need right now, Dwyer. Sorry."

She left me staggering and stammering there, so overcome by desire that all I could do was open my mouth and let spittle run down my jaw.

"God, Dwyer, do you look silly."

"Shit," I said, "shit."

"Very articulate."

"Listen, I—"

A shadow crossed her face and she smiled gently. "I want it, too, Dwyer, I really do. But not now, okay? God, after my divorce I used to hop in the sack with almost anybody who'd ask me, but I kinda lost sight of me in that process, you understand? I want this to mean something because I really kinda like you. Even if you are still in love with Jane."

I started to respond to her last statement, but I still hadn't found my tongue. Anyway, I didn't know what I felt for Jane anymore. A lot of things—confusing things—maybe nothing more than duty. I wanted to help her out of her predicament with the police, I knew that. Beyond duty, though, I wasn't sure anymore. . . .

"Why don't you ask me what I found out at the bank?" she said.

Finally I could feel desire slowly, slowly leave me. I said raspily, "Yeah, what?"

"Boy, that was good. 'Yeah, what?'"

She made me laugh, and I loved it. "Okay, what did you find out at the bank?"

"That an older woman came in, handed over cash, and took a certified check."

"Cash?"

"Cash."

"This older woman—" Then I explained to her what the Branigans had told me about the older woman in the art gallery. Who was she? What did she have to do with all this? Was that who Carla Travers had been on the phone with when I was there?

She whistled softly. "Maybe that's who I should start checking out."

"The older woman?"

"Yes."

"You may make it yet."

"As a journalist?"

"Among other things."

"If I put my arm on your shoulder and kiss you on the cheek, will you promise not to grab me?"

"I'm going to have to think it over."

"I'm serious."

"So am I."

I thought it over. "Okay. But make it fast."

"Here goes."

She leaned over and kissed me. I wanted to grab her. I didn't.

"That was sweet," she said.

"If you say so."

"What a jerk."

During our little romance here I'd made up my mind to something. "I have to go," I said.

"Where?"

"You keep trying to find something out about the older woman."

"And you're going to be doing what?"

I shrugged. "Nothing much," I said, "just a little breaking and entering."

GETTING IN TOOK FOUR GOOD MINUTES WITH A wedge of flexible metal I had borrowed one time from a stoolie I'd known during my policeman days. Four cold minutes, thanks to the wind.

There was an official smell to Elliot's house now, a residue of the chemicals the ME and the lab people had used during their investigation.

Even dark, the place was still ridiculously big and the antiques ostentatious. I didn't know where to start so I elected the most obvious room, the library.

Fir branches scratched the windows behind the curtains, casting shadows like the fingers of dead men clawing at me.

Twenty minutes later I had spread several curious items from his desk drawers on the floor and was looking at them with my flashlight.

'CULTURE' IS NOT A DIRTY WORD
TO THIS AD MAN

Stephen Elliot, the thirty-nine-year-old creative director of Hammond Advertising, and the man many acknowledge as being the number-one advertising force in the city, is eager to tell you that he prefers classical music to rock, Ingmar Bergman to Alfred Hitchcock.

"I proudly admit to being a snob," the darkly handsome ad man says. "If you watch my commercials carefully, you'll see that I manage to work in a bit of classical music in each one—or even the image of a serious painter or two."

Elliot cites his award-winning work for the I'm Chicken fast-food chain and the Go Fast car-rental agencies as examples. Both campaigns feature classical music motifs as part of their novelty.

Elliot is credited by many in the advertising community with having saved the Hammond shop from bankruptcy. When he joined the firm it had lost millions and was widely assumed to be on the brink of final collapse.

Elliot's ideas, according to these insiders, turned Hammond's fortunes around.

For all his brashness, Elliot is oddly reticent to discuss the things he's done for Hammond. Of Bryce Hammond, the agency president, he says, "Bryce is one of the legends in our business. He's brilliant."

Elliot is as much in demand as his commercials. His messianic style, seductive and evangelical at the same time, has made him popular on the speaking circuit—and, many insist, the boudoir circuit as well.

Unwilling to speak about his past except with the vaguest of generalities, Elliot remains something of a mystery even to those who claim to know him well.

"I am my work," he says passionately, a hint of anger in his voice. "I am the Picasso of my business—and that's how I want to be judged. By my work and nothing else."

If he weren't being buried tomorrow, I would have laughed out loud, or at least smiled at his pretentiousness. But I was beginning to see that that was part of his mystique—his archness. Advertising people would love it—accustomed as they were to the boorishness the field seemed to promote. He looked good in a dinner jacket and muttered a few phrases of French and didn't tell racist jokes over lunch. What more could you ask for?

The rest of the stuff in the drawers was mostly a collection of odds and ends, love letters written to him—fortunately for my ego, I didn't find anything from Jane—innumerable tear sheets from newspapers and magazines with articles about how wonderful he'd been, a framed high-school graduation photo of himself, and finally one of those little cards that come attached to flowers. This one read: "To Buddy, who has taught me far more than I have taught him. All my love. Eve." Then there was a high-school pennant that said, "Grovert Tigers."

Finally, I found a small green phone book, a Yellow Pages for the city. On the cover was a name—Eve—with a local phone number. I tore off the section with the number and put it in my pocket.

I clipped off the flashlight and sat back against a leather couch and thought about everything.

If I were reasonable at all, I'd go with the police wisdom and just say that Jane did it. I'd found her with what was presumably the murder weapon in her hand. She'd been out here, she certainly had motive, and she was presently in a state of shock, a circumstance not exactly unknown to killers overcome with remorse and terror.

But there were troubling and unanswered questions. Where had Stephen Elliot gotten all his money? Who was the older woman at the art gallery who'd slapped him? What was the real nature of the relationship between Elliot and Carla Travers, a woman he could not possibly have considered as a bedmate? And what about David Baxter? In the restaurant that afternoon he'd denied killing Elliot—but what else would he say? There was even Bryce Hammond to consider, though why he would kill Elliot was impossible to guess. Elliot had literally been his meal ticket.

My mind went back to the mysterious older woman. Where could I find her?

Going along with the police was beginning to get

tempting. Their version of the murder seemed to make the most sense.

I decided to waste a few more minutes. I brought my flashlight up and peeked inside an unpromising white envelope.

Even by today's standards the photographs were startling.

The fat man wasn't making love. He was lying back, completely naked, his beer belly riding his otherwise skinny body. He had a beer can in his hand and a silly party hat on his head. His privates were very much at rest. What made him so startling was his grossness—his hairy body, his bald head, his doughy face. He was so real he hurt the eye.

The contrast between the man and the woman was unbelievable—he was so repellent and she so lovely that they might have been of different species. She was naked, too, lying there next to him on the cheap motelroom bed, but even in this scuzzy circumstance there was beauty in her blond hair and lithe body, the breasts small but shapely, the thatch of hair between her legs as tidy as the rest of her.

I had forgotten how good Jane looked without clothes on.

I don't know how long I sat there staring at the photo. I wanted to vomit or smash somebody's face in. Either one would have been all right.

There were other photos in the envelope. The same man with a different woman, a woman who made David Baxter suddenly a viable suspect. The woman was his wife, Lucy.

14 I TRIED TO THINK OF HER IN THE HOSPITAL, tried to think of her as I'd seen her in the park when she'd called me a few days ago and shown up holding a gun. I tried to relate both these images to the woman I'd just seen in the photographs and—I couldn't. I had never imagined there was a side to her like that and a part of me still refused to believe it, insisted the snaps were faked. But I knew better, of course; I knew better.

Stuffing my pockets with various things I'd gleaned from Elliot's desk, I let myself out again, back to the numbing air that acted now to cleanse me. What I was beginning to learn, and suspect, about Elliot was starting to make me hate him. Then I thought of Jane again, how she looked in the lurid light of the amateur photos, and all I could feel was pity—for her, for me, for her parents if they ever found out.

I got in my car, backed out of Elliot's curving driveway, and headed for the only man who could answer the questions I now needed to ask.

Hammond Advertising is located on the top three floors of one of these bunkerlike buildings architects are so proud of these days, or at least that generation of architects who have confused function with ugliness. Squat, square, a tribute to concrete, it sat in the center of an island of asphalt, purple except for an occasional lighted window in its twenty stories, the purple of mercury-vapor lights.

The lobby was empty except for a mannish woman bent over, shining windows. Neither of us seemed especially happy to see the other.

I took the elevator up, got off, and stepped into a darkness in which I could make out the shape of a splashy reception area.

I was in a kind of frenzy, looking forward to seeing Bryce the way I'd look forward to seeing a priest. I had to unburden myself of what I'd found tonight. Feelings of love, hate, sorrow—I needed to talk to somebody.

The floor seemed limitless. I walked past dozens of inky office doorways. Scents of everything from tobacco to perfume to artist's glue to cleaning solvent floated at me like phantoms from the shadows.

An odd noise stopped me a moment. I had a sense that it was an alien noise in this environment, but I wasn't sure why. I looked left, right, beginning to sweat for no reason. I sensed eyes watching me from the gloom. Then I heard a more familiar noise—the peculiar booming sound a 16-mm motion-picture projector makes. I moved toward it through the gloom.

I opened a door into a screening room, where Bryce Hammond sat in a theater-style seat in the luminous arc of the projector light. Thick blue cigar smoke coiled like snakes through the light. He was laughing so hard he didn't notice me.

On screen, in a black-and-white commercial that dated from some time in the midsixties, a wimpy man with a big hammer was destroying his lawn mower, pounding it into rubble. "Do what you've always wanted to do to that mower of yours—then come down and get a genuine Cartwright mower." The final scene was of the guy standing on his dead mower like a white hunter on a carcass.

Another commercial started to run within seconds of this one, but I cleared my throat so that he'd notice me.

He glanced up, seeming strangely embarrassed. "By God, Dwyer, c'mon in!"

He punched a button on the arm of his chair. The screen darkened and the houselights came up.

"You caught me," he said. "I was screening some of my old commercials for a client, some of the ones that won the Clios. I guess I take an inordinate pride in the work I did when I was—hot." He waved an arm. Laughed. "You're wondering where the client is, right? He's off taking a leak." He stared at me. "You all right?"

"Not right now I'm not," I said. "I need to ask you some questions."

His brow knitted, his handsome face grew serious. He nodded for me to sit down.

"Care for a beer?" he asked.

"Yeah. That sounds good."

He went over to a wall panel, stepped deliberately on the floor, and the panel opened to reveal a dry bar. He took two bottles of imported beer from a small refrigerator and brought one of them over to me.

"Thanks."

"You bet. Hell, you look like you could use it."

I decided to get on with it. "What can you tell me about Stephen Elliot's sexual tastes?"

He was obviously surprised by my question. "He was a lady-killer as far as I know."

"No rumors to the contrary?"

He smiled. "There are always rumors to the contrary, you know that. Everybody thinks everybody else is queer, just as the old Quaker saying has it."

"But nothing ever substantiated?"

He swigged from his beer. Even in a brown suit he

seemed better suited to the deck of a yacht than an office. He shrugged. "No."

"What about his background?"

"His background?"

"Yes, where did he come from. What college did he go to? Where did he get his agency experience?"

He eyed me levelly. "Forgive me for saying so, but you seem a little—Well, why don't you try just sitting there and relaxing? You look like you're going to jump down my throat if I say the wrong thing."

"There's something very wrong here, Bryce."

"Like what?"

"Like the way Elliot spent money. You admitted he couldn't have made it all from advertising."

"What else?"

"His relationship with an older woman—nobody seems to know anything about her. Just that she fit into his life somehow. Know who I'm talking about?"

If he was lying, he was good at it. "No." He paused. "Why did you ask me about his sex life?"

I had come here to take him into my confidence, to use him as a combination friend-shrink, but now I realized that I couldn't, that I owed it to Jane to keep the photos secret.

"Why did you ask?" he repeated.

"I heard something."

"What?"

I paused, seeing I was getting exactly nowhere. I made a show of relaxing. I even smiled. "I think maybe you're right, Bryce. I think I'm a bit overwrought."

"Hell, man, that's easy to understand, what with Jane— well, you know." He leaned forward, swigged his beer again. Then, "If it'll comfort your mind any, I think Elliot was as straight as a ruler. He liked women too much to be anything else."

He had just gotten done reassuring me when the door to the screening room opened and a man walked in.

The man came over in his country club-style western

clothes and when Bryce introduced him as Phil Davies, he shook my hand as if he were trying to choke it.

"Nice to meet you," I said, and then I turned to Bryce, cuffing him on the shoulder. "I appreciate the beer and the talk. I guess I'm getting a little strung out is all. You know."

"I sure do." He grimaced. "This hasn't exactly been my idea of a fun couple of days, either. As you know."

We shook hands and I turned to leave. "Nice to meet you," I said with a great deal of politeness to Phil Davies, a bald-headed, doughy-faced man.

Not that I felt any desire to be polite. Phil Davies was the man in the photograph with Jane.

15

THE LAST TIME I'D DONE A STAKEOUT WAS JUST after I'd started with the security company, when I did my one and only bit of husband-following. A prominent black surgeon was seeing a prominent white lady in the media. His wife was not happy. She engaged us to document what was going on. It was not the sort of work designed to enhance your self-image. After two nights I asked to be taken off the job. It wasn't a big deal for my employer. He said all right.

Tonight I parked my Datsun in the shadows of a nearby building, waiting for the sight of Davies.

During my wait I went through anger, depression, and a real curiousity about him. How the hell had a slob like him ever coerced a beauty like Jane into bed? The answer had to be Elliot. Somehow he had convinced Jane to do it. For what reason I couldn't imagine. . . .

Davies came out an hour later, got into a big gray Mercedes-Benz sedan, and drove off. I stayed a comfortable half block behind.

The time was near midnight as we cruised into a shabby section of the city, not quite a ghetto, but working hard at it.

There was no way Davies lived here.

A few times, his driving getting a bit erratic, I wondered if he had suddenly become aware of me. But, no. I decided he was probably somewhat in the bag.

He got a good, long, six-block run going, apparently bored with the sluggishness of his journey, wherever it was he was headed. I had to move to keep up with him.

Five minutes later he pulled onto the driveway of a motel named the Palms. Red neon from the electric palm tree bloodied the macadam. The lights from the office made the front window look greasy and dirty.

What the hell was a man like Davies doing here?

He got out, his unsteadiness as he swung his foot free indicating that I'd been right, he was a tad potted. He waddled into the office in his cowboy sheepskin coat and pounded hard on the bell.

The man who appeared was tall, skinny, and dressed in a sort of disco style, with a too-snappy white suit and an open white shirt. He did not look pleased to see Davies. The two of them went behind the counter and disappeared into a room on the right.

I sat across the street and watched the cars go by, the noisy teenagers driving rock 'n' roll missiles, the older people in rusted and busted vehicles that could scarcely pass safety inspection. Inside a slob rich enough to drive a big Mercedes was doing God knew what with an aging parody of John Travolta.

As I said, I sat and waited. There was nothing else I could do, much as I would have liked to.

He came out after another hour. He was moving even more unsteadily now. He cracked his head getting into his car, then drove off, jerking and uncertain.

I let him go. I had a sense that the motel clerk could be helpful if I made him so.

The Palms was a four-story job with rusted iron railings running along the exterior hallways on each floor. Salesmen for tightfisted companies would stay here, and working-class high-livers cheating on their spouses. Again, Davies's visit made no sense.

The office smelled of grease from an empty sack of hamburgers that sat on the desk.

David Letterman was talking to a vivacious guest, deftly putting her down and making her like it, and my friend, the forty-five-year-old disco guy, was enjoying it.

I hit the bell with the heel of my hand hard enough to startle both the clerk and myself.

"Why don't you hit it a little harder?" he said. "Maybe you'll win a prize."

He came over in a cloud of Brut and hairspray, one of those gangly, vaguely criminal specimens who hang out in nightspots and occasionally get busted for small crimes. Once in a while booze or drugs or plain animal heat gets the better of them and then they commit a big crime, usually murder two, and spend several years getting hit on by cons.

This specimen wore several rings, a toupee at least one size too small, and a chain around his neck that could get you through a snowstorm in winter. He stared at me with a mixture of contempt and fear. He must have sensed that I wouldn't mind smashing his face in.

"A fat man in cowboy clothes came in here about an hour ago," I said. "I want to know why."

Nobody his age, which I put at close to fifty, should have giggled the way he did. The noise gave him a hillbilly aspect that collided with his disco getup. "You really think I'm going to answer you?" He shook his head with real pity, as if I'd just asked the ultimate dumb-shit question. I noticed he was already reaching for the wall phone behind him. It was unlikely he was going to call the police. I wondered just who his contact would be.

"Don't touch the phone."

"Huh?"

"You heard me."

He was sensible enough to drop his hand.

"What was he doing here?"

"Who?"

Now it was my turn to laugh. "Who? Phil Davies, you asshole."

He shrugged. "Just stopped by to have a brew."

"Right. You and he are undoubtedly good friends. You probably give him clothing tips and like that."

He glanced at his white suit as if I'd just insulted not only his mother but his wife and children as well.

"You got something against my clothes?"

"Yeah. A lot."

He glowered.

"Davies. Why was he here?"

He started to reach for the phone again.

This time I grabbed him hard enough to give myself a small thrill. I pulled him even with the desk and threatened to jerk him over it.

"Hey, shit, c'mon." I could tell he was worried about his clothes.

"Why was he here?"

"Jesus, man. Let me go, all right?" He was scared and kept pawing for the phone.

I decided to emphasize my point.

I dropped him, then I went around behind the desk and took the phone off the wall. This was nothing that required strength or brains. It snapped right off its holder, the way Ma Bell intended. I threw it in the wastebasket.

"Hey. God, man. Hey." He was babbling. I had succeeded in astounding him. The sweat on his face was as bright as the rings on his fingers.

"Hey, yourself, jerkoff. Now answer me."

He sighed. Touched a hand to his face. A trembling hand. "He gets laid."

"What?"

"He comes here and gets laid."

"Who does he screw?"

"Usually some chick named Jackie."

"Where do I find her?"

"Not sure."

"Bullshit."

I said it sharply enough that his boozy eyes got nervous again.

"Really," he said.

"She got a pimp?"

"Uh-uh. She's only part-time. I think she's a model or something."

I looked around the office. At the girlie calendar. The black-and-white TV set. The couch that was sprung and filthy. I couldn't imagine a model working out of here.

"What kind of model?"

"Over at the Triple XXX."

I couldn't help myself. I laughed. "You call that 'modeling,' huh?"

"Yeah, that's what they say on the marquee, asshole. 'Live models.'"

"Right. Just like Cheryl Tiegs."

"Who?"

"She's a model. A real one."

"Oh, yeah? Nice tits?"

I just shook my head. "Was Jackie here tonight?"

He hesitated.

I put some mean on my face.

He sighed again. He was getting as tired of the game as I was. "Yeah. Yeah, I guess that was her."

"Where would she have gone?"

The way his eyes flicked—for just a moment and to the left—answered my question.

"What room did they use?"

But he had gotten silent again. I reached over and started to grab him, but he backed up and held up a hand to stop me.

"Two-two-three," he said.

"You sure about that?"

"Yeah. It's the room they always use."

"Give me the key."

"She's got it. Knock. Just say Larry sent you."

Clever material. 'Larry sent me.'"

"Fuck you."

And that was how I left him.

From various rooms I could hear TVs and laughter, and from one the sound of lovemaking. With the wind swallowing it all up, everything sounded lonely and futile. The door to Room 223 was ajar. I prodded open the door with my toe, felt to my left, and clipped on the light.

Larry hadn't been kidding me. Jackie was there, all right, naked and striking a seductive pose across the rumpled bed.

The only trouble was that, with a great deal of precision, in an act apparently long on skill and short on passion, her throat had been slashed. Blood was soaking the sheets around her and giving her poor, small breasts a curious kind of Indian war paint.

AFTER I CLOSED THE DOOR I WENT BACK
downstairs to the office. The clerk was just
hanging up the phone when I got there.

I went behind the desk, grabbed him, threw him onto a
chair.

Then I told him about the dead woman upstairs. As I
spoke, I watched his face. He seemed honestly shocked,
and then afraid.

"Shit," he said miserably, "shit. They're gonna blame
me." You could hear the tears in his voice. "I'm goin' back
to the slammer for sure."

Usually I wouldn't have had the stomach for it, as I don't
take any particular pleasure in the misery of others, but now
I just leaned against the back of the desk and watched him.

He lit a cigarette and jumped up and started pacing. He
looked seedy and mean and vulnerable all at the same time.

"You killed her, didn't you?"

"Jesus Christ," he said, whirling on me. "No, I didn't. I
really didn't."

"You've got a record, don't you?"

"Yeah, but for B and E. Nothing violent."

"You know how cops are. Suspicious of you no matter what you did time for."

He wiped sweat from his face. Lit another cigarette.

"You need a buddy," I said after a time.

Now he was into the depressive side of his manic run. He stared out the front window at the cars that crept by.

"You need some help, Larry," I said.

"Yeah," he said, dully. Jane had sounded that way the other day in the park.

"But if I'm going to help you, I've got to know what was going on here."

"Yeah."

I went over and picked up his pack and put another cigarette in his mouth. I even lit it for him.

"I don't want to go back to prison," he said. He sounded about eight years old, with the boogeyman loose in his midnight bedroom.

"Then tell me the truth."

He shook his head. "I'm as scared to tell you the truth as I am to go back to the slammer. You saw what happened to that whore upstairs."

"Who did it? Phil Davies?"

"I'm not sure."

"Why was she killed?"

"Because she knew."

"Knew what?"

He exhaled smoke. With red neon splashing his beard-stubbled face he looked like a prisoner already in hell.

"Knew what, Larry?"

"Knew what was happening."

"What was happening."

"She posed for pictures for some guy."

"What kind of pictures?"

"You know. With bottles and fruit and stuff up her. That kind of stuff."

I thought of the photos of Jane and Phil Davies. "Any other kind of pictures?"

"Whaddya mean?"

But I had a feeling he knew exactly what I meant. "Any other kind of pictures—with men while another man was watching?"

"Kinky stuff?"

"Yeah."

"I suppose."

"You know a man named Stephen Elliot?"

He said it quickly and badly. "No."

I smiled. "I thought we were going to be buddies, Larry."

"Honest. I never heard of no Stephen Elliot. Honest."

I decided to crack the whip again. "What do you think I should do about the dead woman upstairs, Larry?"

"Shit, man, they really will blame me for it."

"Right."

"I don't know what to do. Fuck." He was talking to his tortured self.

"I can help you."

"How?"

"I know the cops pretty well. I used to be a cop myself."

He looked me over. "Really?"

"Really."

"You got good buds on the force?"

"Good buds, Larry. Good buds."

"You really gonna help me?"

"Yeah, if you help me."

His eyes began to look worried. "Like how?"

"Like tell me who you were talking to when I came in just now."

He tried another bad lie. "I was ordering a pizza."

"With anchovies, huh?"

"Yeah. With anchovies."

"Deep dish, I'll bet. Those are the best kind."

"I love fucking deep dish, man. I love the shit."

I hit him so hard his head cracked back against the wall and his knees started to buckle. Then I brought my knee up and caught him squarely in the groin. I let him slide, screaming, to the floor. I sat down on the chair next to where David Letterman held court and watched Larry try to pull himself together.

He was in bad shape. He had been all his life. I wasn't proud of what I'd done to him just now.

I sighed. "Larry, be smart. For your own sake. Call the cops. Tell them everything you know. Everything."

He looked up at me. An eerie, bitter smile was on his face. "You know, I always thought I'd turn out better than my old man did." He shook his head miserably. "I fucked everything up just the way he did."

Then he went back to holding his crotch and groaning.

Outside I got in my car and headed for an address I'd found in the residential directory back in the office.

Phil Davies probably didn't like receiving guests at this time of night, but right now I didn't care a whole hell of a lot about his feelings.

17

STONE PILLARS SAT ON EITHER SIDE OF A driveway wide enough to take a circus caravan. The estate was maybe six prime acres. In the foggy moonlight ahead I saw a rambling colonial home that easily put Davies in the upper 2-percent income bracket of the city. His Mercedes-Benz sat in the drive where it curved past the house. A four-stall garage gleamed white through the murk. Beyond the garage was a tennis court, tarpaulined for the winter.

I parked, crunched over tiny pieces of gravel to the broad porch, ascended the steps, and used the brass knocker to rile the night.

The harsh noise it made embarrassed me. Probably Davies had a wife, maybe even children still living at home, and this was going to be terrible for them.

A woman wearing big pink Martian hair curlers and a flannel bathrobe opened the door. "Yes?"

"Are you Mrs. Davies?"

"I'm Myrna, the maid."

"I need to speak to Mr. Davies."

She peeked outside to his car. Then she peeked at me.

"I'm afraid he's asleep."

"I'm afraid I'm going to have to ask you to wake him up."

I succeeded in making her angry. "If you're not off this porch and out of this driveway in one minute, I will be calling the police."

The slap of slippers sounded on the polished floor behind her.

Davies, formidable in his robe and looking not a bit sleepy, appeared behind her.

He seemed shocked when he saw me. "Aren't you the fellow I met at Bryce's tonight?"

I nodded.

"What the hell are you doing here?"

"I need to speak to you."

"About what, for Christ's sake?"

"The Palms."

There is no other way to describe it—his face died. Human light left his eyes and his mouth went slack. He looked old and beaten.

"We'll be all right, Myrna," he said in barely a whisper.

"But—" She was still angry, even if he wasn't.

"Please," he said.

After another scowl in my direction she left.

He led me inside and across an expanse of floor to a door on the right of the grand staircase.

Inside was a den such as Ronald Colman might have had in an old MGM movie. There was a single twist. Instead of being filled with traditional culture—busts of composers, matched first editions of Henry James and Herman Melville—what he had here was a repository for artifacts of the American West. From the elk horns displayed on the far wall to the beautifully framed Frederic Remington paintings, this room was a tribute to pioneer days.

He still wasn't speaking. He went over to an impressive bar and poured great amounts of bourbon from a decanter into glasses. He brought me mine, then sat down in a thronelike leather chair. He indicated for me to sit too.

Then he did something quite surprising. From the pocket of his robe, he brought out a revolver and aimed it directly at my face.

"You have five minutes to explain why I shouldn't kill you." He waggled the gun. "And don't think I couldn't get away with it. In case my house doesn't convince you, let me say that I am a very powerful man in the city."

I said it simply. "The woman you were with tonight is dead. Somebody cut her throat."

The way he started, I could see that it shocked him. "Bullshit," he snapped.

"It's a little late for me to come out here with made-up stories."

I had the impression the gun was going to fall from his hand. He sat there with his wide body looking tough and in charge, but suddenly all his strength seemed to leave him.

He said, to himself, "She had a little girl. She showed me her picture once."

"Larry, the night clerk, is probably going to implicate you in this. If I were the DA, I'd assume you killed her. I followed you from Hammond's tonight, right to the motel. There wasn't a ten-minute lapse from the time you left to the time the body was found. That would mean somebody had to have moved pretty fast. That kind of thing happens in movies, but almost never in real life."

"What the hell were you following me for?"

My anger started to return as I had to explain myself. I took the photo of him with Jane from my pocket and flashed it at him.

"Recognize this?"

"Of course I do," he snapped. "I've been paying for it for several months now."

"Paying?"

"I assume you know how blackmail works." His sarcasm conveyed his anger.

"If I'd known that that bitch was—"

"I'm going to give you an opportunity to take that back. I happen to be very fond of this woman. Very fond."

He sized me up, then decided to back off. At least a bit. "We had a little fun together. A little 'casual nudity,' as I call it. We didn't even do anything. Just—" He shook his bald head. He was on the verge of becoming an old man. Tonight was hurrying the process along. "I guess I'd better tell you about my wife. She suffers from heart disease. Her doctors feel she could die at any time. They've warned me against stress or any kind of emotional upset where she's concerned. She's been in bed for the better part of the last six years. I know this may smack of rationalization, but I need a bit of life too. So I—play around—nothing very serious. The—woman—tonight—Jackie. We have our fun, but she's actually a decent woman. Just happens to be a prostitute is all."

He gripped the gun more firmly. It was once more pointing at my face.

"Anyway, I need some kind of life. One night after a party at Bryce's, I met—Jane. We ended up at the Palms, rolling around on the bed. It was all pretty silly. As I said, nothing happened. Then the photographs started coming in the mail—you can imagine what they'd do to my wife."

"How much did you have to pay?"

He became cognizant of the gun. He looked at it, at me, put it back in his pocket. Then he put his hands over his face and started shaking his head. Anybody else I would have suspected of crying quietly. But not him.

He looked up at me and shrugged. "When I was young I always thought that at sixty-five I'd lose interest in sex. But it's just the opposite. Now it's assumed a monumental importance in my life. I've retired from my aviation company except for the board work I do and— Sex is still very, very important. That's why I liked Jackie so much. She was patient and kind and very good for me."

"Yes."

None of this made sense. Jane part of a blackmail ring?

"How much did you pay?" I asked again.

"Three thousand a month."

I whistled.

"But you never found out who was sending them?"

"No," he said, "and it's a good thing I didn't."

"Why?"

"Because I would have killed them." He shrugged. "It wasn't the money, it was the potential harm it could have done my wife if she'd ever opened the envelope by mistake." He sighed. "And now—if I'm implicated in all this—"

He sounded very different from the man who'd earlier bragged about how important he was in this city.

The knock almost got lost in the wind. A tiny knock.

Davies swung his large head around and stood up instantly, putting a finger to his lips for silence.

He opened the door and a frail, once handsome woman came delicately inside.

He put an arm around her, and it was easy to see in this gesture how much he cared about her.

"I heard all the noise, honey," she said, "the voices at the front door downstairs and—"

Then she saw me and I was afraid she was going to faint.

The angles of her face drew even tighter and she looked nervously to her husband for an explanation of my presence.

"This is an old friend of mine, darling," he said. "His car happened to stall a few blocks from here and so he decided to walk over and phone a garage from here."

His eyes begged me to leave.

I stood up, walked over, took the lady's hand. "A little piece of bad luck. Sorry I had to disturb you."

"Oh, that's all right. I've become an expert where bad luck's concerned, I'm afraid." She was so drawn and gaunt I didn't mind her self-pity.

"Well," I said, clapping Davies manfully on the shoulder, "the garage truck will probably be there by now. I'll walk back."

"Good luck," he said.

I looked at his wife and then at him. Somehow I didn't hate him the way I had when he'd only been a man in a picture with Jane.

"Good luck to you," I said. I think I was being sincere.

18

"I SHOULDN'T HAVE DONE IT," I SAID.

"Sssh."

"You don't deserve me inflicting myself—"

"Please, Dwyer. Don't talk, all right?"

We sat in Donna Harris's living room and watched rain slide down the front window. A streetlight gave the sight a silver beauty.

I had come here after leaving Davies's. After seeing the picture of Jane, after the death of the prostitute, I felt unclean in some way I didn't know I'd ever recover from.

Like a homing pigeon, I had a sense that Donna could help me with her kind of neurotic strength.

I told her everything, and she listened patiently, and afterward she turned out the light and we sat on the sofa, where we were now, watching the rain.

"It's all getting crazy," I said. "None of it makes sense."

"Sssh."

She held me for a long time and after awhile a kind of rocking motion set in between us and through the depression I felt myself responding to her again. This time she let me put my hands on her breasts and her tongue found mine.

When she stopped me I understood.

"We should wait for a better time."

I couldn't disagree.

In the silence, in the darkness, she lit two cigarettes and dispensed them.

"I found out one thing about the older woman," she said.

"What?"

"She and the Baxter woman you told me about got into a violent argument in the Conquistador one night."

"Where did you hear that?"

"From the parking-lot attendant. Apparently the older woman was waiting by Elliot's car. The Baxter woman pulled in and they got into an argument."

But right now that information didn't interest me half as much as holding Donna did.

This time it was my turn to help her. She started to cry; I wasn't sure why, though she talked about her husband a bit and how life seems to let you down sometimes, so I put her on my lap and she curled against my chest and finally went to sleep.

I got a blanket from the bedroom and put it over her there on the couch and left.

I DIDN'T SLEEP UNTIL NEARLY DAWN. WHICH was when the phone rang. I was groggy enough that the call could have been part of a dream.

But I took what the voice said seriously and got up and got dressed and headed for the hospital after shaving, brushing my teeth, and taking what my parents always called a "sponge bath." Maybe I would have saved time showering.

Edelman, who had involved himself only to help me deal with the Branigans, waited for me in the lobby. We rode up silently to Jane's floor and got off. In the dim light of the elevator I watched my old friend, good cop, good husband, good father, good man. He was getting older. It was like the flu—getting older seemed to be going around these days.

Malachie, the detective officially in charge and the man who'd directed the cleanup at Stephen Elliot's house, stood above the Branigans, who sat on a couch in the waiting area.

Obviously he had just given them the news. The ballistics report was in on the gun I'd taken from Jane that day in the park.

Maybe it was the earliness of the hour, maybe it was because the past few days had drained them, maybe it was because they'd expected it—whatever, the Branigans had taken the news with a kind of bitter quiet. Their expressions were angry, but they said nothing, simply watched Malachie as if he were some kind of rodent.

Edelman touched my arm before we got over there. "I only called because they look like they could use a friend. I know her father's a big-shot lawyer, but—" He shrugged. "I kinda feel sorry for them is all."

"Yeah. I appreciate the call."

We started across the room to them. On my way I saw a story in the morning paper that made me wonder if I wasn't hallucinating. I reached for the paper tossed on the empty chair just as Mrs. Branigan began sobbing.

The sounds were horrible, animal noises and froze everyone in position.

Then Mr. Branigan took her and brought her into his arms, and Edelman and I finished our walk over to them.

"Please, would you mind leaving us alone?" Mr. Branigan said to the officers.

They nodded, proceeded to withdraw. I turned away too. Mr. Branigan said, "Would you mind staying?"

I wanted to see the paper, make sure that I hadn't imagined what I'd seen. But I could hardly refuse him.

I watched as he sat his wife down and put her hands together and fluffed a pillow and put it behind her head for her to lean back against. Apparently the hospital put feather pillows out in case you had an overnight vigil.

Mrs. Branigan, now obviously in bad condition mentally, shut her eyes and began to weep silently and convulsively. Her whole body moved to some ancient rhythm. She was mourning a daughter who was, in many respects, already dead.

Mr. Branigan walked me several yards down the hall and around a corner.

"You know what the police just told us—that Jane is being formally charged with murder." His Spencer Tracy stature, boozed out though it was, bore the dignity of righteousness just then. He was professionally angry.

"They're charging her with murder in the first degree, if you can believe that."

I didn't know what to say, do.

"I hope you've been looking into this," he said.

"Yes. I have."

"Have you learned anything?"

"Nothing I can talk about right now."

He kept his eyes on me. "What do you think?"

He had confused me. "About what?"

"Now that my wife's not here, be honest. Do you think Jane killed him?"

"No."

"You don't sound as sure as you once did."

About that I couldn't argue. The more confusing things got, the more anything seemed possible. Even Jane's complicity in murder.

He said, "Do you need money?"

I didn't want anything from him. I felt sorry for the Branigans, but we'd never been close, so why should we start now? I shook my head.

"I'm not impressed with either of those cops. Malachie or Edelman." He smiled unpleasantly. "Lord spare me from Jewish policemen." I'm sure the line would have gone over very well at his country club.

"Edelman's a good man."

"I'm sure he is, 'good' that is. I'm not so sure about his competence."

I sighed. "Look, I realize she's your daughter, but think of it from their point of view. She calls me hysterical, I meet her, she has the murder weapon in her hand, and then she slides into shock. That would seem to indicate guilt, or at least a heavy involvement."

He wanted to change the subject. "What do we really know about this Elliot? I met him once. He struck me as a little—faggy. I can't quite explain it. But there was something about him—"

"That seems to be the concensus. Not gay—just strange in some way." I nodded to an orderly who was walking by.

"The other thing we seem to know is that nobody is sure about his background. I've asked Bryce Hammond for his résumé, which he's supposed to get me. And one more thing—Elliot lived way beyond his means."

"That was the impression I got when my wife and I visited them in his house. My God, *I* could hardly afford a place like that. I didn't see how he could, no matter how 'creative' he was."

"I'll keep working."

He offered me his hand. "You know, we were talking about you last night."

I knew what he was going to say and I wished he wouldn't.

A common goal was making us friends, and I always distrust friendships that aren't more spontaneous in some way.

"We've decided," he said, "that we were very wrong about you and we're very sorry."

"Well, thank you," I said, "thank you very much."

We walked back. A nurse was giving Mrs. Branigan a glass of water, helping her drink it.

Edelman came over. "The DA thinks he's got this one wrapped good and tight," he said after I'd waved good-bye to the Branigans and was walking to the elevator.

"He's wrong."

There was pity in his eyes. "Shit, man, you gotta be kidding. I know what she means to you, but—"

I got on board the elevator, tilted my head good-bye, watched as the doors closed.

Then I opened the newspaper I'd picked up.

MOTEL CLERK KILLS PROSTITUTE, SHOOTS SELF

Larry the clerk had been wrong about one thing. He said his life was just as screwed up as his old man's had been. It sounded as if, right at the last, he'd managed to make his even worse.

20 DO YOU EVER DRIVE AROUND TO THINK things through? There's something about motion that inspires concentration, even if it doesn't exactly make you into a wonderful driver.

God knows I had enough to think about. In my cop days I used to make a simple list of all the people involved in a homicide investigation. That was on the right margin. On the left I made another list, their possible reasons for wanting the victim to die. I could see it was time that I do that.

On top of Stephen Elliot's murder—and now the deaths of the motel clerk and the prostitute, which had been disguised by somebody very clever as the murder-suicide the press was reporting—there was my growing confusion about Donna Harris. Last night had been a downer of sorts and I wasn't sure why. It wasn't just because I'd dropped in unannounced and she'd been sleepy. I felt a sense of her holding back. Maybe it was simply because I was rushing things out of my own needs. Or maybe there was something going on. . . .

When I got back to my apartment, the hour-long drive having made me think through things to the point of quiet madness, I found a message from Donna with my answering service.

"She left an address," the operator said. "Would you like it?"

I wrote it down, a terrible feeling starting to form like a weight in my stomach. Maybe Donna was taking this detective thing seriously. Maybe she'd started to investigate on her own and gotten into some trouble.

"No phone number?" I asked.

"No, just the address."

"Thanks."

Fifteen minutes later, having violated more than a few traffic laws, I wheeled into the parking lot of 2605 Kelvin Avenue.

The large brick complex had originally been designed for swank office space. But the city built an expressway and bypassed the place, and now the offices were anything but swank. The owner spent minimal dollars on upkeep, and the space that had been designed for suites now housed a myriad of tiny, struggling businesses. Half the insurance agents in the state seemed to be here, along with a number of firms with totally baffling names such as "Omega Corp." Maybe the obscurity was intended.

I took an elevator to Room 402, as Donna's message had instructed, to find myself in a hallway with carpeting that was shaggy from wear, not by design. Everything looked chipped and scratched and dented. It was unlikely the Getty family would consider leasing space.

There was a hand-stenciled sign on 402 that said AD WORLD. WALK IN.

Which was what I made the mistake of doing.

The first thing I noticed was the couple holding hands. Right then I didn't know who the guy was, only that he had Donna's hand cupped in his and was staring fondly into her eyes. He was a tribute to razor-cut hair and camel's-hair topcoats and the kind of bearing meant to intimidate. His

Gregory Peck head turned slowly and irritably to take note of me.

Donna flushed, pulling her hand from his more quickly than he probably liked.

"Gee, Dwyer, hi."

She was redefining the word *strained* for our generation.

"Gee. Hi." I wasn't doing much better.

"This," she said, "is Chad."

Then she nervously jumped to her feet and came around the desk and sort of clapped me on the shoulder. "Chad. The former Mr. Harris."

By now he had walked around the desk too. Unlike Donna and me, he seemed to be feeding off this moment of general embarrassment.

He put out a hard, dry hand politician-style and I shook it.

"So you're Dwyer." He shook his head. "Donna's told me all about you. You sound like quite a character. Part-time actor, part-time private eye. Quite a character."

Why did I feel that I was standing for inspection before Donna's father instead of her ex-husband?

And he was making it clear that I had failed inspection. *Quite a character* is one of those phrases that could fit anybody from Howard Cosell to Jack the Ripper.

He looked around the tiny office as if he were a land baron inspecting his domain. Everything seemed slightly humorous to him. Not because it was funny, but because it failed his standards in some way. His dark eyes danced with smugness.

"It's nice you're going to help her with her little magazine project," Chad Harris went on. *Little magazine project* irritated me. I could see that he was good in court. The best lawyers have that ability to undercut and deflate with subtle language. The good ones rarely go for the bombast. Chad here could castrate you with adjectives.

Before I could respond, he tucked his thumbs in his vest and strolled around the room as if he were a tour guide in a museum. "She's done a wonderful job, don't you think?"

And she had.

She'd covered the walls of the one-room office with framed copies of her best ads. They lent color and style to the place. The inexpensive filing cabinets were new enough to shine and the round coffee table around which she'd placed three straight-backed chairs gave the room a sense of proportion. Only the glum wintry sky filling the cracked window spoiled her work.

"Great job," I said. But I still hadn't found my voice. All I could think of was them holding hands. Who had a better right than formerly married people? But that didn't help, of course. My mind had outstripped the reality of Donna and me. There was nothing between us, certain sappy thoughts of mine to the contrary.

"This should generate a nice little income for her," Chad was saying.

"Chad was nice enough to lease this office for me for six months," Donna said.

"Boy, that's wonderful," I said. "Just fantastic." Maybe I should have tried "absolutely and totally fabulous" or something while I was at it.

Chad glanced at his watch like a surgeon inspecting a liver. "Damn. Late for court."

His hand struck out again.

We shook.

He shrugged into his camel's-hair coat and surveyed the office again, and then did what I'd hoped he wouldn't. Leaned into Donna and put a possessive arm around her waist and a more than perfunctory kiss on her cheek.

"Don't forget about dinner," he said. "That's a forsure, toots."

Then he beamed at me magnanimously and I sensed, as I always sense around men like him, all the ways I have failed not only my gender but the fucking human race, and then he did me the inestimable favor of opening the door and leaving.

We stood in the kind of silence that only lovers can share. Part suppressed anger. Part hurt. Part confusion.

"Gosh," she said.

"Gee," I said. And pointed out all the things that had just been pointed out by the one and only Chad. "This looks great, fantastic." There I went again—fabulously wonderful, et cetera.

"So," she said.

"So."

"You got my call."

"Got your call. Yes indeed."

"Were you surprised?"

"To put it mildly."

I knew she was talking about *Ad World*'s office space so once again I waved my arm in the direction of the ads hanging on the wall. "Fabulous," I said.

Then she decided to give us both a break. "It was kind of uncomfortable, huh?"

"Yeah."

"I didn't expect him to show up. He just kind of popped in and—"

"Hey, you don't owe me an explanation."

"Well, I do sort of Dwyer. I mean, we're in a weird situation here, wouldn't you say? I mean, we're not really lovers or anything, and neither of us really owes the other anything, but there is something going on between us, don't you think?"

"Something. Yeah."

"So here I am holding hands with my ex-husband when you walk in."

"Yeah. I noticed that."

"Your eyes bugged out. Sort of like a cartoon character."

"God, was I that obvious."

"I'm afraid so."

"Shit."

"It's all right, Dwyer. I don't handle things like that very well myself."

I sat down and lit up a cigarette, confused and miserable. "Maybe it's better if we don't talk about it."

She lit up too. "Yeah."

"So this is really a great office."

"The last time you said it was fantastic. In fact, you've alternated between fantastic and fabulous. Great is sort of a step down."

"Oh. Okay. This is a fantastic office."

"Yeah. I really like it."

"And it was damn nice of him to lease it for you." I wanted to cut out Chad's heart, of course, but there didn't seem to be any graceful way of working that into the conversation just now.

"Fabulous of him, actually," she said. Then she said, "And it was a complete surprise. He calls one week to see how I'm doing—I mean, we're really good friends these days—and tells me to meet him at this address in half an hour—and *voilà, Ad World* has its first office."

"He really seems like a fantastic guy."

"I thought he was a jerk."

"That's what I thought you thought."

"I mean, if we're being honest."

"I understand."

"He kind of sneers."

"I know."

"And he puts people down."

"I kinda figured you didn't like being called 'quite a character.'"

"Also I didn't like him calling this your 'little project.'"

"That's how he was all the time we were married."

I was a fucking lapdog, but I couldn't help myself. I just wanted her to say something reassuring about us. "I can see why you broke up."

"He's dumping the court stenographer."

"Oh."

"He says he thinks he's in love with me. He says he

thinks he never really fell out of love with me. That the thing with the stenographer was just a middle-age itch."

"Well," I said.

"I thought I'd better tell you that."

"I appreciate it," I said.

"You don't look like you appreciate it."

"Well, I can appreciate it without being absolutely fucking thrilled about it, can't I?" The anger was starting to surface.

"I really like you a lot."

Man, I could hear it coming. I wanted to beat her words to the door.

"Right now I'm just confused," she said.

"Right."

"I still want to work with you and—and maybe even see you, you know?"

"Yeah."

"But right now . . ." She paused.

"Yeah, I know."

"Shit," she said.

"That seems to be as good a word as any," I said.

I left.

21 MALLEY'S IS THE ONLY BAR I KNOW WITH A crucifix in plain sight of the drinkers. Bob Malley, a paunchy, bearded guy I made my first communion with, keeps it near the cash register in case a fight breaks out. Over the years he's gotten his nose and jaw and left arm broken. This, in his own bar. Now when he jumps between two brawlers he takes his crucifix with him, sort of like Darren McGavin fighting off vampires on "The Night Stalker." The weird thing is, it works, mostly because Malley's customers consist of innumerable mumbling Irish Catholics in various stages of psychosis. It's like having a nun appear out of a booze fog and threaten to work you over with her steel-tipped ruler.

Malley also doubles as a highly opinionated shrink. I tell him my troubles mainly to hear him tell me what a messed-up jerkoff I am. I told him all about Donna and her husband. Malley just snorted at me pityingly and walked away. He was going to formulate a plan for me. I started drinking beer.

Barbara Mandrell came on the jukebox and then B. J. Thomas and then George Jones. None of them made me feel any better. Malley had this thing for country music now. We used to listen to Dion and the Belmonts.

I knew there was only one hope for salvation. I needed to be working again. I took out the piece of phone book I had ripped off at Elliot's place. The one with the name "Eve" on it.

Eve seemed to have some central connection with the death of Stephen Elliot and Jackie the hooker. Not to mention Larry.

I went back to the pay phone, slugged in some coins, and got a surprising response.

The line was busy.

I'd been expecting the number to be no longer in service. The busy signal buoyed me. I felt some forward progress.

Kenny Rogers and then Willie Nelson stirred the beery air. Malley used to be a stone rock 'n' roll freak. I couldn't believe what he'd done to his jukebox. Country music was not my favorite type of music.

Throughout this miniconcert I kept trying the number again. Busy. I went over to the bar and got four quarters for a dollar. I'm at least as superstitious as your average Druid. I figured maybe new coins would unbusy the line. Right.

"You know what you need, Dwyer? A girl from St. Michael's," Malley said. "Find somebody from our old class—shit, man, they're all divorced now—find one of those babes and start plugging her and get married. Find somebody who cooks good and likes to give head. You make things too complicated."

He shook his head at me as I walked away. As if I were the numero uno dumb shit. Crude as he was, and God, was he—to the point of embarrassment most of the time—maybe he had a point after all. Maybe I should find a woman from my own background. Maybe that was my trouble. But I kept remembering the last such date I'd had. How she'd kept telling me dirty jokes all night and how she got wine-sappy over Eddie Rabbit records. Despite Thomas

Wolfe, you *can* go home again: it's just that there are very few people there you want to see.

"I beg your pardon?"

He sounded like a bad dinner-theater actor imitating British gentry.

"Eve," I repeated. "I'd like to speak to Eve."

It had taken me half an hour of changing between dimes and quarters—and half an hour of a regular Grand Ole Opry tribute on the jukebox—but finally the line had cleared, and I asked for Eve.

Only I got this guy. With his accent. With his ice.

"I'm afraid you have the wrong number," he said. "Sir." He added the last after a two-beat pause, and the way he said it was a masterpiece of subtle venom.

Then he hung up.

I tried to put the phone somewhere deep within the wall on which it hung.

Malley must have been watching me, because when I got back to the bar he said, "Believe it or not, Dwyer, Ma Bell makes me pay for shit my customers break."

"Sorry."

He waved his bar rag at me. "You won't fucking listen, ma. Won't fucking listen."

He slid a brew toward me.

"I know," I said. "Good eats and good head. Right?"

He gave me a WW II thumbs-up sign. He didn't look a damn thing like Harrison Ford. Which is fortunate for Harrison.

Somebody named Lee Greenwood came on the jukebox. It was getting to be time to leave.

"I got somebody you should meet," Malley said.

"Let me think about it."

"Don't forget your origins, man, that's what it comes down to." Yeah, I thought, I want to live in a housing development with fake-brick walls in the basement "rec" room and "naughty" paintings in the bathroom, which is a fair description of Malley's place.

Then I felt like a jerk and a snob and I wanted to confess to Malley that I was both those things and that I was sorry and that he should pay no fucking attention to me, drunk or sober, whatsoever.

But I didn't.

I just kind of nodded good-bye, pushed through the smoke, and found the back door. I'd parked in the rear because there was usually a slot there. Tonight that proved to be a mistake.

I stood for maybe two or three minutes finishing my cigarette. Then, not wanting to go back inside and have another conversation, I decided to relieve myself next to the dumpster.

They were there all along, of course. Only I had no way of knowing that.

Steam rose off my work and I rocked on my heels, my head still spinning, and the cold was like being reborn into a terrible gray world from which there was no escape—

And that was when they appeared.

They emerged from the blackness like shadows. They wore dime-store Halloween masks, one a Frankenstein, the other a Dracula. One carried a crowbar. The other wielded a long piece of pipe. Nothing fancy, which meant they were street types. Which scared me. Pros rarely take pleasure in what they do. Street types sometimes get carried away.

I was just getting my pants zipped when one of them, Dracula, swung the piece of pipe.

It made a *whooshing* sound as I ducked under it.

I had found my balance, all right. The problem was that Frankenstein had worked his way to my left. Now he was coming up from behind.

I was already sweaty. Nerves. And a tic worked my right eyelid. Nerves. I started to yell for help and that's when Dracula, who was much better at this than I was, made his move. He came straight for me, and I had no choice but to answer him.

I brought my right foot up and caught him in the groin, but he grinned despite his pain.

Frankenstein came from behind—a crunch of gravel, a muttered curse in Spanish—and brought oblivion with him, swinging the crowbar exactly against the middle of the back of my head.

I went out. Absolutely out.

22 IN MALLEY'S THAT NIGHT I BECAME A celebrity. Everybody had to come up and look me over. There was a couple in square-dancing clothes and a couple in polka clothes and a couple in evening clothes of the sort Lawrence Welk probably had wet dreams about. There were racists—"You can bet they was fuckin' niggers"; philosophers—"Hey, man, you're alive, thank God for that"; vigilantes—"I say we get goddamn grenade launchers and go after those sonsabitches." There were ladies who wanted to commiserate—"Malley tells me your old lady dumped you, huh? I ain't doin' nothin' tonight"; and ladies who didn't seem to want much of anything at all—"My ex-husband, he spilled his motorcycle, he hurt his head just like that, yeah."

That was how I spent the next four hours of my somewhat dubious life, propped up in a corner under a TV set while ESPN reran an Ali fight from 1971 and the announcers had to pretend to get excited all over again.

Every few minutes Malley came by and said, "I still think I should call the cops."

"I appreciate the offer, but I'm all right. I don't feel like sitting in a station and filling out forms."

He alternated between wanting to call the cops and wanting to call an ambulance. According to him, he knew the signs of concussion, so several times he shined this searchlight-size flashlight into my face and started mumbling doctorlike things to himself. The square dancers and the polka folks and the evening-outers all crowded around and kibitzed on my condition.

He was halfway through his fourth such number with me when the phone rang and he had to reluctantly put down the light to answer it.

He shoved a finger in an ear so he could hear and then surprise parted his lips and he pushed the phone to me.

"It's for you," he said.

Moving still hurt so I took my time. Right after waking up in Malley's alley, I'd figured the mugging for a coincidence. Then slowly, as my senses returned, I knew better. By now I was half expecting this call.

I took it. Put my own finger in my own ear. Dolly Parton was singing now.

"Yes," I said.

"You got a hard head, meester."

"Yeah. I must."

"We went easy this time. Next time—no."

"Mind telling me what you've got against me?"

By now Malley had caught the drift of the conversation. He made a theatrical gesture to a guy behind the bar who himself made a theatrical gesture out of picking up a double-barreled shotgun and handing it to Malley.

"You tell that cocksucker to come over here," Malley said. Malley's face looked like somebody who'd gone crazy in a panel of a *Sergeant Rock* comic book. All he needed was a stubby cigar hanging out of the corner of his mouth.

"You lay off the investigation you got going, man," the voice on the phone was saying. "Otherwise we're going to lay on the hands again. A lot harder. You dig me?"

He was doing a bad imitation of a juvenile delinquent in

an old Glenn Ford movie. At least he hadn't called me "chickie baby."

I handed the phone to Malley.

Before the poor bastard on the other end hung up Malley had insulted the guy's father, mother, sister, brother, *and* dog.

"Here," Malley said after slamming the phone.

He presented me with the shotgun as if he were a king sending his most trusted knight into battle.

I thanked him but declined the offer. The police department probably wouldn't be too happy to see me riding around with a shotgun in my car. They just don't have the sense of humor most normal people do.

This time when I got outside all that was waiting for me was the realization that I was totally alone. A veritable hunchback of self-pity.

IN THE MORNING I STOOD INSIDE THE SHOWER long enough to get Simonized. My head, surprisingly, didn't feel too bad unless I touched the goose egg itself.

The first thing I did after dressing was check in with my answering service. A Dr. George Chamales had called. So had Donna Harris. At the mention of her name my heart did several silly things. Then I thought of Chad-the-charmer and felt outleagued.

I decided to call Dr. Chamales and worry about Donna later.

He had a voice that could easily put me out of a job. Med students all seem to take drama courses these days. They're much smoother than the previous generation.

"I'm the psychiatrist working with Jane Branigan," he explained. "I feel we're making very rapid progress. I wondered if you could come in and see me in the next day or so. Perhaps our having a conversation would help."

"Is she talking yet?"

"Not speaking on the subject of the murder, if that's what you mean. But she is coming out of shock. We're very optimistic. She's a lovely woman."

His remark about her loveliness caught me in an odd way. I realized then that I no longer loved her, at least not as I once had. There was an emptiness in me now and I almost missed the pain of grieving over her.

"Yes," I agreed. "She's also an innocent woman."

"I'm afraid the police have a fairly convincing case."

"That's because they're not looking at any other facts," I said. Such as a dead hooker named Jackie and a clerk named Larry. "I'll try to get in tomorrow. I'm afraid I'm busy today."

"That's fine," he said. He sounded as if he were absolving me for not rushing right over.

From the funeral section in yesterday's newspaper, I'd gotten the home address of the dead prostitute, Jackie.

She'd lived in a section of tract homes that looked small enough to be fishing cabins. In the overcast morning their faded colors ran the spectrum of dead dreams. Even the toys in the front yards were rusted. The sidewalk was swollen and cracked. I knocked on a tinny-sounding aluminum door.

The woman wore black hair dye, a yellow sweater that bound up her sagging breasts, and enough malice in her brown eyes to start a small war someplace. She was maybe fifty and damn unhappy about the fact.

Of course, what interested me most was the black eye that ran in a semicircle under her left eyelid.

"Yeah?"

I showed her my license.

"So?"

"I'd like to talk to you."

"I ain't got it."

I had been there long enough to feel the effects of the smell. She'd made herself something greasy for breakfast. It lay on the air like the odors of a slaughterhouse.

"Got what?"

"You think I don't know shit, don't you?" she said.

"Maybe we'd better start over."

"The cops wanted it, then this prick who called in the middle of the night, he wanted it too."

"Wanted what?"

"Shit," she said.

"I really don't know what you're talking about."

"Jackie's book."

"What book?"

"The phone book with the names of her customers in it."

"Oh." This was beginning to make some sense now. "You mind if I step in?"

"Yeah. I do mind."

I took a twenty from my wallet. "Will this help?"

She looked at it skeptically. "My frigging daughter gets stabbed to death and all you're offering me is a frigging twenty?"

I had underestimated this lady's sense of status. Two twenties was the price of admission.

The house looked as if it were a nuclear testing site. In front of a TV set watching cartoons was a miniature representation of this woman. Jackie's daughter. The kid didn't even look up.

"So, like I told you, I ain't got it," she said.

"Mind if I ask how you got the black eye?"

"I thought you were interested in Jackie."

"I am. But I'm also interested in your black eye."

"I tripped against a cupboard."

"Right."

"I don't give a shit if you believe me or not."

The little girl turned around. Looked at me. "Are you one of Mommy's friends?" she asked.

"No, hon, I'm not."

"Good. Mommy's friends weren't nice."

"Shut up, Sandy," the grandmother said.

Sandy shrugged, turned around, went back to Scooby-Doo.

"I got to go to the funeral parlor and make plans," the woman said. "So hurry up."

"Did your daughter ever mention a man named Stephen Elliot?"

"No."

The way she said it, so fast, so bold, I knew it was a lie.

"How about Phil Davies?"

"No."

Same impression.

"Did she ever discuss her—business with you?"

"Gee, you can say it, mister, unless you're some kind of frigging altar boy. My daughter was a hooker. You try to live on AFDC sometime and see where you get. Nowhere is where you get."

I took out another twenty. This was like playing a very expensive slot machine. "I'd like to know where her phone book is myself."

Just then the phone rang. Grandma swore and stalked over to it like a stevedore going to pick up a three-hundred-pound crate.

The call seemed to be one of sympathy. "Yeah, you just ain't safe nowhere these days," Grandma said.

I drifted over to the TV.

Sandy sat amid the mess. The couch was tattered and sprung in several places. One armchair had only two legs. The TV was an Admiral.

I sat down on an ottoman stained past color recognition.

"That used to be my boy's favorite show," I said, "until his tenth birthday."

"Yeah. Scooby's my favorite."

I smiled. "What other shows do you like?"

"Oh. Scary ones, you know."

"Like what?"

"Oh, "Nancy Drew" and "Batman." They're good ones."

"You like being scared, huh?" I smiled.

"On TV I like bein' scared. Not in real life, though. Like those two guys who came here last night."

"Two guys?"

"Yeah. They hurt Grandma."

Grandma was watching us and listening and was obviously not happy. To the phone she said, "Hey'm Phyllis, I gotta hurry, okay?"

"Who were the two guys?" I asked Sandy quickly.

"I don't know. They wore masks."

I took a shot at it. "Dracula and Frankenstein masks?"

"Yeah. They were really scary."

Grandma slammed the phone and came over. "What the hell you been tellin' him?"

She kicked Sandy in the buttock. Not hard enough to hurt, but hard enough to make her point.

"One of them hit me with a crowbar," I said. "They're not people to take chances with. I assume you gave them her book."

She glared at me. "You assume what you want." She flung her arm toward the door. "Get out."

I nodded good-bye to Sandy and started my way back through the debris.

"I hope for your sake you gave them the book, otherwise they'll be back."

"You're damn right I gave them the book. I saw what happened to my own daughter, didn't I?"

I looked back at Sandy, a child already so lost no amount of social programs could ever reclaim her.

"So long, Sandy," I said.

She didn't acknowledge me. She was back to Scooby-Doo. It was all she had.

I spent an hour at a casting for a walk-on part as a daddy in a pizza commercial (I've got a pretty good daddy-style grin). They'd let me know. Of course.

Then I called the security service I work for and talked to my boss, who must have bathed himself in Preparation H because he was actually in a decent mood. I wanted to find out if the store I was working in was happy with my work. He said peachy-keen.

Finally I got to my real work. I drove over to the phone company and looked up a balding guy I'd known from my days on the force. He was an executive now and had the pinkie rings to prove it. But we liked one another and each did the other favors whenever possible or necessary. He took Eve's phone number from me and went to check it out. He came back twenty minutes later and said, "A hotel suite. Posh fucking territory, my friend. Unlisted number and the whole nine yards."

Half an hour later I stood ankle-deep in carpeting in front of the manager's office at the Wyatt-Smythe hotel, the only luxury place left in the loop. They overdo their image. I wouldn't want to have illicit kicks in a place that comes on like a cathedral.

The manager was the new breed. No longer do they try to resemble Adolphe Menjou. Now they're Corporate America. This guy could be a prosperous word-processor salesman. Gray flannel suit and all.

He was my age and infinitely brighter. He didn't seem haughty, just comfortably superior. He didn't invite me into the office. I wasn't important enough. He talked to me standing by his receptionist's desk.

"I'm working on an investigation," I said.

"Oh. You're a policeman?" He knew better. He just wanted to impress the receptionist."

"Private."

"I assume you have a license."

"Of course." I showed him.

His receptionist tried to see it too. Probably just curious. He handed it back to me. Then I handed it over to her. I thought it was kind of funny. He didn't laugh. She smiled, anyway, with cute little baby teeth.

"How may I help you?"

I showed him the phone number. "This is the number of the penthouse."

"It seems to be. Yes, indeed."

"I need to know who was in there last night."

"Why?"

"As I said, I'm working on an investigation."

"It's not our policy to divulge things like that."

"I can always bring the police in."

"Exactly what does that mean?"

I shrugged. "I'm doing you a favor. This is a non-official inquiry. No publicity of any kind."

"Why would there be any publicity?"

"If you knew what I was investigating, you'd know why there would be publicity."

I tried to make it sound as ominous as possible.

He sighed. "Helen Dodson is the lady. Older. Wealthy. One of our best clients, and has been for many years."

"Nobody named Eve?"

"As I said," he reminded me tartly, "her name is Helen Dodson."

"Does this Helen Dodson have a servant?"

"I wouldn't call him a servant, exactly. That's a little ostentatious. More like a man Friday, I would say."

"Is she up there now?"

"I'm afraid she checked out."

It was becoming obvious that Eve and Helen Dodson probably had nothing in common. The number I'd gotten from Larry-the-motel-clerk's phone book could have been written down months earlier. This was the kind of wrong turn you got used to as a homicide detective.

"I wonder if I might have her address?"

He looked startled. "Mrs. Dodson's?"

"Yes."

"Why?"

"To be honest, I'm not sure."

"I'm afraid I can't help you." He consulted a wristwatch worth enough to feed any small African country. "And I'm also late for an appointment. Good day, sir."

With that, he was gone.

The receptionist smiled at me as soon as he disappeared. "Why don't you wait here a minute?" she said.

I watched the pleasing shape of her hips work against the fabric of her tweed skirt as she walked over to one of those formidable filing systems that rotate.

A few minutes later she was back and handed me a slip of paper.

"Here's Mrs. Dodson's address."

"Thank you," I said.

"I've never met a real private eye before," she laughed. "Wait till I tell my son."

Around two that afternoon I pulled into a quiet residential street that dead-ended on a few acres of timberland. In the assault of cold wind only the houses—mostly brick two-stories that only doctors and accountants could afford—looked warm.

The large white wood house with the captain's walk that sat on the edge of a ravine belonged to Mrs. Helen Dodson.

After a heart-attack lunch in McDonald's, I decided that checking her out might be worth the trouble. If nothing else, it would eliminate her from future consideration.

The call from Dr. Chamales had given me my edge back. The police planned to push Jane Branigan as their one and only suspect—without looking at any other possibilities.

The brown grass on the edge of the driveway leading to the Dodson house was frozen from an earlier rain. I sensed rather than saw somebody staring out at me from one of the windows. I went up and knocked. Getting no response, I rang the bell. Then I knocked again. The grim day chafed. A collie came up, looking cold. He inspected me, then passed on. Still no response from inside, even though I was sure somebody was in there.

I tried the bell again. Nothing.

I decided to commit the unpardonable sin in suburbs such as these. I walked across the grass to the next house.

A stout woman in a housedress whom I took to be a maid—she was dusting—saw me from the front window and opened the door before I reached it.

"Hi."

"May I help you?" she said. The welcome wagon would probably never hire this woman as a representative.

"I need a little information about the Dodson house."

"My employer isn't home. You'd need to talk to her. Anyway, I don't know nothing about Mrs. Dodson."

"You know how long she's lived there?"

"Why?"

I showed her my wallet.

"I don't know nothing about Mrs. Dodson," she said. Then she closed the door.

The collie I'd seen earlier was jumping around a panel truck that was just now pulling into the Dodson driveway. A uniformed delivery man got out and brought a package to the front door. From the green wrapping, it was easy to see that he was bringing flowers.

There was something off about the sign painted on the side of the truck. It read WINDOM'S FLOWERS, TANROW.

Tanrow was a small town maybe forty miles from here. In this age when florists wired their flowers, why would a truck drive forty miles for a delivery? The guy got in his truck and pulled away. I started after him, yelling.

He must have had his radio up full blast. Didn't hear me. He went down the block with me running after. I could see all the people in their living-room windows, looking at me. Probably they'd soon be calling the cops. It was a good time to get out of there.

I was too distracted by too many things to do much of a job watching shoplifters that night.

I tried, of course. I spent a full hour trailing two teenage girls who came awfully close to getting a hair dryer out the door—but they finally figured out who I was and gave up. A pro came in, a three-piece-suit type of pro, and we thrusted and parried for the better part of two hours. When he decided to call it quits he stood near the entrance door and offered me a smile and a salute. I sort of saluted back.

Without knowing why, I kept thinking about the flower truck from the town of Tanrow. Damn long drive. Of course, I had other things to think about—such as Jane Branigan in the hospital waiting to regain her full faculties so the police could arrest her. And Donna Harris lying abed, as the poets say, with Chad the charmer.

Then the call came. There couldn't have been any call in the world that would have surprised me more than that one.

24 "ANYWAY." DONNA HARRIS SAID, ANGLING her Chevrolet into a parking place outside the Hilton located along the river, "I figured it would be a good excuse to see you. Plus we can check out all the suspects."

Earlier tonight I'd had Donna, in my mind, ready to remarry her ex-husband. All she'd tell me was, "Maybe I'll tell you later." She'd said that while she'd waited for me in my living room as I changed from work clothes to a suit and tie. We were going, at her expense, to the Addy Awards, the local ad club's annual bash.

Now that we were there, I realized that I was likely to irritate more than a few people tonight, among them Carla Travers, David and Lucy Baxter, and probably even Bryce Hammond. Private detectives had a way of spoiling festivities.

The wind chewed at us as we entered along a wall of glass that revealed a poolside party. Perhaps as many as two hundred people in tuxes and evening gowns stood by the water, holding champagne glasses and making like windup toys with little bursts of laughter. Were they really having as good a time as they seemed?

116

She took my hand.

"You mind?" she asked.

"Not at all."

"Good."

Her words made me feel ridiculously happy. Her perfume did the rest of the job, seducing me despite the chilly, starless night.

Only a few people seemed interested in us as we descended the steps. The combo in the corner kept right on playing what seemed to be a disco version of "My Funny Valentine" (I do not lie).

"Hey," several people said to her.

Donna smiled and said "Hey" right back. ("What the hell is 'hey' supposed to mean?" she asked. "I think they pick that stuff up in places like Altantic City and Vegas," I explained. "Yeah, along with crabs.") We found drinks—bourbon for me, scotch for her, though she admitted this would be her one and only hard liquor drink for the night—and then we danced two or three times in the deepest shadows we could find. I held her tighter than I should have for public view and she held me back just as tight. I lost myself in the clean smell of her red hair and the tang of her neck as I kissed it.

Then she said "God!" as if she'd discovered oil and I realized then that she'd touched the goose egg on the back of my head. "What happened to you?"

So I told her about the punks at Malley's bar. I tried not to sound too much like Clint Eastwood saying it was nothing, but I'd honestly forgotten about my head until she mentioned it.

Then I told her about the threatening phone call afterward.

"Well, that clears Jane Branigan, doesn't it?"

"It does for me, anyway."

"Well, won't the police agree with you?"

I shrugged. "Not necessarily. A good cop would just say

that the mugging and the phone call were a coincidence. That they were talking about some other case."

"What other case?"

"It wouldn't matter. Since the punks didn't mention Jane, the police would still insist it was all a coincidence—or at least that I needed a lot more proof for them to pay any serious attention."

She frowned. We had gone back to dancing, but now we held each other at arm's length so we could talk. "My first issue's got to be finished a week from today. I talked to the printer. I haven't been doing a very good job, I'm afraid."

"A wonderful job."

She stared at my eyes. "You're getting dippy, Dwyer."

"Thanks."

"I'm serious. Don't placate me. I'm doing a lousy job. I haven't even found out about who the older woman was in Stephen Elliot's life."

I told her about the penthouse and the phone number and Mrs. Helen Dodson and the flower truck from Tanrow.

"Jeez, I really appreciate being clued in like this," she said.

"You upset?"

"A little bit, yes."

I couldn't resist. "Well, maybe you'd find these things out sooner if you spent a little more time with me instead of your ex-husband—"

"Up yours, Dwyer."

She sulked for the rest of the dance—kind of a swing version of "The Impossible Dream"—but by the time the combo did their fox-trot rendition of "Jumpin' Jack Flash" she held me tight again.

The lights had dimmed. The din had dulled. I was struck by how much this reminded me of a high-school prom for chaperones. We were all a little long in the tooth, but we had the same approaching-midnight needs—the ache for fleshly solace, the easing of daily terror, the soothing grace of whispers. I pulled her tighter and then she said, "I'll tell you about it, if you want."

Actually, I'd been trying not to think about it. Not with a lot of success.

"It's none of my business."

"You really don't want to know? I mean, I'm in kind of a bind here. If I don't tell you what happened between Chad and me after dinner last night, I'll feel as if I'm mistreating you—that you aren't important enough to level with. But on the other hand if I tell you—"

"Maybe you'd better not."

"Seriously?"

"Yeah." I had an image of her in his arms. I wanted to lose that image.

"Nothing happened."

"Bullshit."

"You don't believe me?"

"You wouldn't tell me if something had happened between you."

"Sure I would. That's the whole point of bringing it up, Dwyer. So that we'll get used to telling each other the truth."

"Nothing happened? Really?"

"Really."

I smiled and we went on dancing.

A few minutes later she interrupted my bliss again by saying, "Now that I've told you about Chad, how are you feeling about Jane Branigan these days?"

"I want to help her get free of this murder rap."

"Besides that, I mean."

"I like her."

"How about love her? You still think you love her?"

"That's the weird thing. I don't think I do anymore."

This time she pulled me tighter and we stayed that way for a long, long time.

* * *

Half an hour later we opened the doors leading to the main ballroom, which was presently all got-up in a nightclub motif. Tiny lamps on tiny tables gave the room a European air while on the long stage a master of ceremonies was handing an award to somebody. The three or four hundred people in the ballroom applauded. It was nearly eleven. They had been applauding for almost three hours.

We took a table in the rear, ordered martinis from the waiter, and sat back to watch the ceremonies for a while.

"They always leave the important awards till last anyway," Donna said, lovely in the lamplight. On our way up here she'd plucked an orchid from a vendor's display and set it jauntily behind her left ear. I wondered if she knew how good she looked to me.

For the next ten minutes a screen that appeared magically from the top of the stage was filled with examples of commercials. Not one of them starred me or anybody I knew, even though they were all local. So much for vanity.

Even without me, many of them managed to be very good—by turns funny, warm, instructive. Unfortunately, their makers detracted from the commercials somewhat—accepting the awards with a great deal of arrogance or smugness or artsy posturing.

Several acceptance speeches later I was worn down. Much as I like acting, close proximity to show-biz types dispirits me. They make me want to hang around plumbers or farmers or guys who fix flat tires. There were too many in-group jokes and far too much credit given and taken. They were honoring people who made TV commercials, for God's sake, not brain surgeons or missionaries.

"You look mad," Donna said.

"This is getting depressing. All these berserk fucking egos."

"You are mad."

"Yeah."

Then I saw Carla Travers.

Even in a chiffon evening gown she still looked like a

lady who could wheel a semi around an icy corner. Still looked like the lady who'd brained me with a gun in her apartment. She walked a tad unsteadily and there was something sad about her beefy shoulders and the mannish gait to her walk. I thought of her abortion story, how the jukebox had played while the baby was being ripped out, and I thought of her odd, possessive attitude toward Stephen Elliot. I needed to talk to her again.

Then something else interesting happened.

Not a minute after Carla left the ballroom so did David and Lucy Baxter. If only one of them had gone, I wouldn't have thought much of it. But two of them made things suspicious, particularly so soon after Carla.

God wanted to make sure I got the point—because a minute after the Baxters passed through the doors, Phil Davies got up from somewhere near the front of the room and left, too, looking different from the night he'd begged me to leave his house before his invalid wife got suspicious.

"Gee," Donna said.

"No kidding."

"Now if I were a detective, Dwyer, would I follow them?"

"Right away."

"Let's go."

The night crew was vacuuming and dusting and polishing when we reached the staircase.

We looked left, right, up, down.

Not a sign of any of them.

"You take the ladies' room," I said.

The men's room was empty. So was a small lounge where a piano player played badly at "Skylard." I tried the swimming pool area. Nothing.

Ten minutes later I found Donna outside the ballroom again.

"So much for my first assignment as a detective," she said. "Zip."

"I've got an idea."

"I'm glad you do."

In the elevator she said, "Well?"

"Well, what?"

"I thought we were working together."

"We are."

"Then how about giving me a clue about what the heck we're doing, Dwyer?"

"You sound kind of drunk."

"I am, but so what?"

"I thought we'd check out the register."

"Why?"

"Well, at bashes like these, guests sometimes rent rooms or suites for private parties."

"Hey, good idea."

She really was drunk.

The night clerk was another IBM graduate. He didn't look susceptible to my private-eye routine so I pretended we were looking for a private party. "Actually," I smiled, "it could be listed under several names. If I could see the register—"

Donna, who was weaving slightly by now, whispered a bit loudly, "Gosh, could you hurry? I really need to find a bathroom."

The night clerk, having heard, looked unhappy. But her remark seemed to convince him that we really were just harmless partygoers. He showed us the register. Tonight Room 708 belonged to Phil Davies. We thanked him and left.

Donna had found a bathroom and redone her makeup and she was walking straighter by the time the elevator let us off on the seventh floor.

"This is fun," she said, "being a detective. I may write the story in the first person."

"Kind of like a private-eye adventure?"

"Yeah. Like that."

"Right," I said doubtfully.

I paused in the corridor, leaned my head into 708, and listened.

Nothing special. Conversation. Ice cubes dropping into glasses. Water running in a sink someplace.

"You ready?"

"You nervous?" she asked.

"Sort of."

"So am I. Only more than sort of."

"It'll be all right."

"I sure hope so."

I knocked.

Phil Davies must have been standing next to the door. He opened it instantly. He stood there in his country-western style tuxedo, a deep brown bourbon drink in his hand and a frown on his beefy face.

"I don't seem to remember inviting you," he said.

Donna squeezed my hand tight enough to grind my knuckles together. She wasn't kidding about being nervous.

"You did." I kept my eyes level on him. "Right after your friends at the motel died."

He nodded angrily to Donna. "Who the hell's she?"

"Donna Harris. *Ad World*," she said. Actually, she sounded pretty good saying it.

"You're a reporter?"

She looked at me as if for confirmation. "Yes, she is," I said, since she couldn't seem to speak for herself, "and a damn good one."

This time she squeezed my hand in gratitude.

Lucy Baxter appeared behind Davies, radiant in a green silk dress that flattered her full breasts.

"Oh, more people? Aren't you inviting them in, Phil?"

"I don't think so," Davies said. He smiled nastily at me. "Riffraff."

"What he means by that," I said to Lucy Baxter, "is that I've never spent a night in the Palms motel."

She looked confused by that, shrugged lovely shoulders, and said, "Oh, don't be a poop, Phil. Let them come in. This party needs a little cheering up." She was drunker than Donna. There seemed to be a lot of that in the air.

She slid a long, graceful arm around his waist and angled him away from the door so that we could come in.

Donna glanced at me skeptically, but I escorted her inside.

And there they stood—David Baxter, Carla Travers, Lucy Baxter, and Phil Davies.

Staring at us.

"Bourbon is fine for me," I said.

David and Lucy Baxter exchanged a murky look, and then Lucy said, "What about your friend?"

"Club soda," Donna said, trying very hard to act sober.

The door leading from the room to the veranda was, surprisingly, open. Who would want to stand outside on a night that was below freezing? Then I decided it must be the heat here. The room was hot. And the moods of the people weren't much different.

"Lovely dress," Lucy Baxter said to Donna. I kept remembering how Lucy had looked in the photograph with Phil Davies—her beautiful, young nakedness contrasting with his middle-aged paunch.

A Nat "King" Cole album started playing on the stereo. "Phil hates rock 'n' roll." David Baxter laughed.

Lucy and David went out onto the veranda. Danced despite the cold. Phil glowered at me and went to the bathroom. That left us alone with Carla.

"One thing, Dwyer," she said. "I've got to give you your balls. You got real guts to be here."

"Kind of an odd little group, isn't it?"

"What's that supposed to mean?"

"Only that I'm wondering what you have in common. Why did you decide to have a party together?"

"Maybe we're friends."

"I don't think so."

She knocked back the rest of her drink and staggered over to the bar for another. She looked fat and sad in her promlike formal. And old.

"Maybe I should take some guesses about what you have in common," I said.

"Maybe you should just get the hell out of here."

"Stephen Elliot."

"What?"

"That's the only thing you people could possibly have in common."

"Yeah, that's what this is, a wake."

I walked over to the veranda. Donna sat on the couch, staring at her hands. This embarrassed her, the subtle, social violence of the confrontation.

"Probably not a wake," I said, "maybe more like a meeting."

Phil Davies appeared again. Carla Travers shot him a warning look.

"What's going on?" he asked.

"Dwyer here is trying to figure out why we got together."

"It's none of his damn business," Davies said. He went to the bar. Refilled. Nat Cole played on. Beautifully. It could have been 1956. I wanted to forget about all this nonsense, dance with Donna. Only an image of Jane in the hospital kept me pushing.

The song ended and the Baxters came back in. The were flushed from the cold night. Lucy said, "Looks like the party came to an abrupt halt."

"Uninvited guests," David Baxter said. He still looked like Paul McCartney, but a malevolent version. He had the swagger you get from walking the deck of a yacht. "Probably time they leave."

"One of you killed Stephen Elliot," I said.

"What the hell are you talking about?" David Baxter said.

"One of you killed Elliot. And a motel clerk and a hooker named Jackie. You also hired two punks to work me over last night."

Davies laughed. "You're real good at trying to pin things on people. The other night I was your prime suspect."

"Maybe you still are," I said.

"Why the hell did you come here?"

"To serve notice," I said. "One of you is a killer and you're not going to get away with it. There's some reason you came together here tonight, some reason I don't know yet. Maybe when I figure it out everything will make more sense."

David Baxter stepped forward. "Go figure it out somewhere else, asshole."

Lucy put a hand on his arm.

There was no point in pushing further. I had done what I'd wanted to do. Whoever of them was the killer would be rattled enough to respond somehow, all I had to do was wait. I planned to call Edelman the next day and tell him all about it and have the police keep tight scrutiny on every one of them.

"Get out of here," Baxter said again.

Donna was up. Pulling me away.

For a moment they froze—like a photograph—the four of them. They did not work at the same agency; they obviously came from widely divergent social backgrounds; they didn't even have age in common. What could have brought them to this room together tonight?

"Come on," Donna said.

As we left the snapshot stayed in my mind. Why were they together tonight?

Near the ballroom, on our way out, several small groups of people stood finishing nightcaps and comparing notes on the now concluded awards ceremony.

"You know," Donna said, squeezing my arm, "I kind of miss being in advertising. I knew a lot of nice people, actually."

This was the first thing she'd said to me since we'd left Davies's room.

"You could always get an agency job again," I said.

She pulled on my arm, stopping me. "I'm just scared, is all. I mean, up there in that room— One of those people probably is a murderer, right?"

"Right."

"God, I just can't believe it."

"Yeah, but think what a great story it will make for *Ad World*."

But her wine-buzzy senses were still reeling. "It's sort of biblical. Cain and Abel. A real murder, I mean."

"Land o'goshin." I smiled.

"Oh, don't be so smug."

I was about to say that I'd leave that to her first husband, but a hand gripped my biceps and turned me partially around.

In his black dinner jacket and black tie, his white mane of hair contrasting with his tanned face, Bryce Hammond was an impressive man. He even knew how to carry a drink just so, like in whiskey ads.

"Your lot seems to be improving these days," Hammond smiled.

"Hi, Mr. Hammond," Donna said. She sounded as if she were about ten.

"'Mr. Hammond'?" he said. "How about Bryce?"

"You don't know who I am, do you?"

"I'm afraid I don't, young lady, but I'm certain I've never met you. I wouldn't have forgotten you."

"Well, actually, you did meet me, Mr. Hammond."

"Outrageous. I don't believe it." He was trying out for Cary Grant.

"I applied for a copywriting job right out of college. You met me in the hall one day and said I should calm down or I'd never get a job. It was really sweet of you."

"Well," he said, "I guess at my age being sweet is about the best you can do."

"Oh, Mr. Hammond."

I was about to throw up. I didn't know who was worse, Hammond for fishing for compliments or Donna for feeding them to him.

A portly, bearded man in a cutaway walked past carrying several Addy awards.

Hammond raised his drink to the man in salute. "Reeves. Good art director. Worked a lot with Stephen Elliot." He shook his head, seeming suddenly unhappy. "With Elliot dead, this will be the last year we win any major awards, I'm afraid."

Donna went at it again. "Oh, but you're a famous copywriter, Mr. Hammond."

"Was, my dear, was."

The portly man was about to have his picture taken and was waving for Hammond to join him.

"Do you mind?" he asked.

"Not at all," I said.

"Nice to meet you," he said to Donna.

She looked thrilled.

When he left she said, "He was really a legend a long time ago. In my advertising classes in college we studied his commercials."

"Then Stephen Elliot came along."

"Don't you think Mr. Hammond ever got jealous?"

"I'm sure he did. But what could he do? He's a realist. His time had passed. Elliot payed the bills."

She shook her head. "The poor man."

"Come on," I said, "or I'm the one who's going to get jealous."

She stopped me as I tugged her toward the door. She touched her head. "Guess what I've got?"

She looked like the "before" part in an Anacin commercial.

"This much alcohol always gives me a headache. I guess I should've told you, huh?"

"Yeah," I said, "huh."

25 ON THE WAY TO THE HOSPITAL IN THE morning I called the security firm I worked for and asked one of the younger people if they'd do me a favor and run a credit check on all the people who'd been in Phil Davies's hotel room the night before. Credit checks lead in all kinds of interesting directions sometimes.

"Hello."

She wore a beige outfit with a mink wrap thrown formally over her shoulders. In the hard, gray, winter light from the window in the waiting room her makeup was caked and her jaw a tad too grim to be pretty.

"Hello, Mrs. Branigan," I said again.

This time she heard me.

She looked up with the eyes of an old woman, a certain bitterness, a certain resignation playing in the mysteries of the irises, like secrets glimpsed through vapors.

She nodded.

"How are you doing?" I asked.

"Oh," she said.

Given the circumstances that was a legitimate answer.

"Dr. Chamales wanted to see me."

"Yes," she said.

"Where's Mr. Branigan?"

"Sleeping. The hospital fixed up some rooms for us. Nice of them."

"Yes, it was."

"She talked to us for the first time last night."

Neither of us knew how to speak to each other with any degree of comfort. We'd been enemies too long.

"I hope you can help her," she said and started crying abruptly. The suddenness of her tears alarmed me. What had Jane told them?

I started over to Mrs. Branigan and was about to put a hand on her shoulder or say something soft, if meaningless, but the old self-consciousness returned and I just stood there, helpless, until my feet took over and led me out of there.

Behind Dr. Chamales was a poster of Albert Schweitzer holding a starving African child. Next to that poster was a signed photograph of Dr. Chamales shaking hands with President Reagan. Go figure.

Chamales was a tanned man—you suspected he vacationed a lot—with a flat, strong grip and a flat, strong face. He had a corncob pipe in the corner of his mouth, a pipe that never got lit and showed no signs of tobacco residue in the bowl. Probably it was a pacifier.

The first two minutes he explained several things in an agreeable and unpatronizing way about trauma and shock and repression. Then he said, "She's very confused."

He was maybe fifty, Dr. Chamales, but right now, despite his tan and his trim tennis-club body, he seemed to slump in his chair. He sighed.

Obviously he wanted to say something. I had to help him.

"Do you think she killed Stephen Elliot?"

He said, "Yes."

"Shit," I said.

"I'm sorry."

"Did she tell you that she did?"

"In so many words. At least, I don't see what other conclusion could be drawn. She—she broke through shock last night and began talking."

"And?"

"Well, what happened that afternoon was this. She called Elliot's apartment around dawn, found him home, and went over there. He surprised her by letting her in. They apparently got drunk together. She'd been taking sleeping pills and tranquilizers during the previous twenty-four hours, which means the alcohol could very well have induced a condition not unlike psychosis. About twenty minutes before she phoned you, she 'came to,' as she phrased it, standing over his dead body with the gun in her hand."

"But if she was drunk—"

He pursed his lips. "Diminished capacity? I realize you're looking for legal angles here, but I can't be very helpful, I'm afraid."

"So it wouldn't be uncommon for somebody in her state to repress knowledge of the actual killing?"

"Not at all. Most of us have a difficult time admitting to even minor faults. Admitting to being a murderer—well, that would be very, very tough."

I nodded.

No wonder Mrs. Branigan had looked the way she had.

"May I see her?"

"I've cleared it with the police for you to spend ten minutes with her. I feel you can help her. She has a very high regard for you. Maybe you can help her find the strength to—face reality, if you understand."

I stood up. He pushed out his hand. "I'm sorry," he said. There wasn't much else to say.

Her hair had been brushed to blonde radiance and her makeup had been applied artfully. If you didn't look carefully at the blue eyes, you wouldn't guess she was doing anything but resting there in the white empty room.

She sat in a cane chair next to a window. She wore a tailored blue robe and hospital slippers. She managed to look both very old and very young.

I had almost reached her before she turned to look up at me.

She said, simply, "Sorry I got you involved in all this."

"I know."

"They think I killed him."

I nodded.

"The thing is, maybe I did." Her cheeks, usually gaunt, looked puffy from tears. Her patrician nose was red from crying too. "The funny thing is, I don't know if I did or not."

"You feel up to some questions?"

"Dwyer, I—"

"You don't need to say anything." I leaned in and kissed her on the forehead. She took my hand and held it, keeping me in my awkward position.

"I really treated you badly, with Stephen and all."

I sat on the window ledge and looked at her. "I've been thinking about that. I don't think it was all your fault. I was pretty crazy from my divorce, pretty demanding—"

Watching her then, I realized for the first time in two years of knowing her that she was actually a frail sort of woman. Her golden looks misled you into attributing to her a self-confidence she didn't possess. I'd loved her so long that somehow I'd never managed to just like her. But I did right now. I liked her very much.

"I don't think you killed him," I said.

"I'm afraid you're in a minority."

"When you called me—when I met you in the park—you never said you killed him. You only said he was dead."

She tipped her head into her hand, shook golden hair. "I just don't remember—"

I asked her to reconstruct the events surrounding Elliot's

death. The details fit exactly what she'd told Dr. Chamales. Especially the part about "waking up" with the gun in her hand, standing over Elliot's body. I'd spent enough time getting lost in a liquor bottle to know how things like that could happen.

When she finished, I said, "I have to ask you something that's going to make us both feel very bad."

"What?"

"I found a photograph of you with a man named Davies."

"Oh, God."

"I—"

I had to give her a long and painful moment to gather herself.

"I don't imagine I'll ever seem the same to you now that you've seen that," she said finally, almost whispering.

"Who took the picture?"

"You know who took it."

"Elliot?"

"Yes."

"Why?"

"He said it would make Davies feel better. Davies always talked about me to Stephen—how attractive he found me. I—" She shook her head again. "For several weeks I refused to do it. But Stephen kept after me—you don't know how he could work on me."

But I knew what she was talking about, of course. There's a certain kind of relationship you get trapped into sometimes that you'll do anything to maintain. I'd had a few of them myself. It wasn't hard to believe that Elliot, who was persuasive enough anyway, talked her into it.

"Anyway, I let Davies pretend that he'd lured me into his motel room. Nothing happened, really. We just took our clothes off and held each other—he was pretty drunk—and then—"

"This was at a place called the Palms?"

"Did Stephen ever tell you what he did with the snapshot?"

"Not really."

"He blackmailed Davies with it."

I guess I'd expected her to act shocked. Instead, she said, "I wondered about that. He asked me to see other clients that way too—but I never gave in. That was one of the things we argued about."

"He found other people to help him." I told her about the photo with Lucy.

"I almost feel sorry for her. She took Stephen from me, but—"

I lowered my head and let her cry for a time. I had deadline pressure here. A cop would soon be knocking on the door. I had to hurry her along while respecting the crushing forces of the moment.

"Did Stephen ever mention a woman named Eve?"

A bitter laugh. Her head snapped up. "The goddess, you mean?"

"I don't understand."

"His mystery woman. I picked up the extension phone one night, heard them talking— At first I thought she might be his mother. She sounded much older. This was early in our relationship. But then I began to see how this woman dominated him in some strange way. Phone calls, birthday cards, postcards from vacation spots—"

"You didn't ask him about her?"

"Or course I did. I got to be pretty jealous of her. I'd get up in the middle of the night and find our bed empty. Then I'd wander into the den and there would be Stephen on the phone. I always knew who he was talking to. Her."

"You don't know where I could find her, do you?"

She shrugged. "I'm afraid not. She really was mysterious. In and out of his life. I tried to find out about her, of course. I followed them everywhere. One night in a restaurant she slapped him. I don't know why."

"What does she look like?"

"Very regal. She must have been extraordinarily beautiful as a young woman. She's in her midsixties now, but she still has an incredibly lovely presence—"

The knock came.

The cop peeked in, wearing an apologetic smile. "Gotta ask you to leave."

I nodded.

"One more quick question. Where did Stephen hide when he took the photograph of you and Davies?"

She looked up. "I think there was one of those two-way mirrors. But Stephen didn't work alone."

"What?"

"Please, sir, if you don't mind," the cop said.

I waved him away.

I couldn't believe what she'd just told me. "Who worked with him?"

"David Baxter. You know, he was Stephen's best friend. He's one of those art directors who are also very talented photographers. That's why I was surprised when you said that there was also a shot of Lucy Baxter. David's pretty cynical, but I can't believe—" The tears started again. "What's going on here, anyway?"

I was just as confused as she was.

ON THE WAY DOWN IN THE ELEVATOR A terrible thought struck me—I had no idea who had killed either Stephen Elliot or Jackie-the-prostitute or Larry-the-motel-clerk. I must have expressed my doubts out loud to myself because the matron standing next to me signaled her displeasure by pursing her lips and rolling her eyes. She probably thought I was an escapee from the junkie ward.

In the wide reception area, through which you passed to the parking lot, a familiar, weary voice cut through the various conversations. I stopped and watched my friend Detective Edelman work his way toward me. He always seemed to be toting an invisible cross.

"I don't know about you," he said, "but I could use a cup of coffee."

The way he averted his eyes from mine, I knew why he was here.

"You arresting her this morning?"

There was a bloodstain on his collar where he'd cut himself shaving. It did not do major damage to his image, however, because Edelman always wore the sort of neckties that clip on, and there isn't a lot worse a guy can do to himself than that.

"Yeah," he said, "I guess you could, uh, say that." He added quickly, "Actually, I'm meeting her lawyer upstairs in about twenty minutes. Everything's going through him. She won't actually, uh, see me, you know?" He frowned. "Hell, Dwyer, I'm going to make it as painless as I can."

"Right," I said, "Kind of a fun murder charge?"

He looked at me and shook his head. "I always hoped we'd never cross swords. You're my friend, Dwyer."

"Fuck," I said. I didn't blame him, but I wanted to blame somebody. I wanted to blame somebody bad. "She didn't kill Elliot."

"How about that cup of coffee?"

I sighed. "Yeah."

During two cups of Sanka—my nerves didn't need any help working toward overload—I laid it out for him, all the suspects, all the strange parts that didn't fit, but that indicated that Jane Branigan was not a very good suspect.

I told him about my visit to Carla Travers's apartment and how she'd hit me with a gun and accused me of breaking into her place the night before ("Why would somebody who sells TV time be carrying a .45?" I asked reasonably enough); I told him about the pornographic photos with Jane and Davies, and Davies and Lucy Baxter, and how Jane had told me that she thought David Baxter had taken her photo ("I mean, right there, Edelman, is a guy with some pretty strong motives—he's in on the blackmail routine and his wife is in one of the photos"); I described Phil Davies and how he'd been at the Palms motel the night the clerk and the hooker were murdered, and how Stephen Elliot had seemed to be blackmailing him ("Just in case you need somebody else with a strong motive," I said, more sarcastically than I needed to); next I related the incident with the two punks wearing the Dracula and Frankenstein masks and telling me to give up the investigation; then I informed him of

Grandma's black eye and how Jackie's daughter told me of Dracula and Frankenstein visiting the house and taking Jackie's phone diary; and finally I described how all the suspects had been gathered in one hotel room last night—and how odd I found it that people who didn't hang around each other, didn't really even know each other, should get together like that.

"I think the phrase, Edelman," I concluded, "is *beyond a reasonable doubt* and I think there's a lot of reasonable doubt where Jane's concerned."

Then he said a very coppy thing. The sort of coppy thing I probably would have said myself if I'd been sitting on his side of the desk. "Hell, Dwyer, I'm not saying she had anything to do with the deaths of the motel clerk or the prostitute. You've told me enough about them that I'm going to rule out the murder-suicide thing and open an investigation. But as for Jane—" He shrugged. "Right now, she's still our chief suspect. Motive, means, and opportunity, Dwyer. I can't get around them—and she's got all three."

"How about the mystery woman? This Eve?"

"What about her?"

"You going to look into her?"

"I don't see where she's got a lot of bearing on the case."

"Dammit, man, she's probably the key."

He made a sad, wan face. He was a good guy. I was flogging him with my own desperation.

We sat there and listened to a Jerry Vale song on the Muzak speakers. It was one of those sunny winter mornings when the light makes everything look almost too vivid—more like a painting than reality. I rubbed my eyes.

"You all right?"

"Yeah," I said. "Thanks for asking."

"Maybe there's something to the mystery woman after all."

He didn't think so. He was being nice. "Right," I said.

"Damn advertising people," he said. "They sure seem

messed up, don't they? The more I know about Elliot, the slimier he sounds."

"But there's a piece missing."

"What?"

"I've heard Elliot described by maybe half a dozen people now, and he seems to have been all things to all people. There's something—" I shrugged. "I don't know. I mean, on the one hand he's this real creative type, very much into his work—which is easy enough to accept—but then on the other hand he's this very dark, scheming guy who manipulates everybody."

"No reason people can't be both."

"I know. But still—"

He glanced at his watch. Tucked a frown into the corner of his mouth again. "It's time."

"Yeah."

I thought of Jane and her parents. Their panic. Fear.

"I'll do it as easy as I can."

"I know."

He stood up, dropped two singles on the Formica. "You find out anything about the mystery woman, let me know."

He was being nice again. I appreciated it.

"Take care, Dwyer," he said.

Then he was gone.

27

I DIDN'T NEED THAT PARTICULAR CALL THAT morning, but it was there nonetheless. My talent agency. I was among the finalists for the daddy in the pizza commercial. "You got a cardigan sweater?" my agent asked.

"Yeah. I got a cardigan sweater."

"Put it on and get your ass over there. The guy from the pizza company's there and he's waiting for you."

The president of Good Times pizza turned out to be a Santa Claus of a man in a three-piece suit. He even had the downy white hair. All the people from the production company hovered around him as if he were about to dispense a map giving the whereabouts of the world's biggest uranium strike. All except the director. He was an arty type I'd worked with once in stock. He liked to give the impression that he hated everybody and everything he worked with. Hell, he'd convinced me of his sincerity a long time ago.

"Daddy Number One," the production assistant announced. This was a blond guy. Troy Donahue twenty years and a heavy beer habit later. The Good Times president kept looking at the guy's belly. Not happily.

When they said, "Daddy Number Three" I got up and walked toward the table where four guys, including the prez, took notes.

"Hi, there. James Todd," the prez said, and we endured a pasty handshake.

He asked each daddy different questions. Kind of a verbal shell game.

"You like Good Times pizza?"

"Really," I said, shamelessly, "it's my favorite."

"What's your favorite topping?"

"Sausage."

He smiled. "Then you should sue us, young man."

"How's that?"

"Good Times is meatless pizza."

I was waiting for the other three guys to turn their thumbs down. Then somebody would open the gate for the lion.

"I see," I said.

He shook his head. "You got eight points out of ten until you opened your mouth, young man."

"I must've been thinking of some other kind of pizza."

One of the production people said, "Daddy Number Four just came in, Mr. Todd."

I took my cardigan sweater and left.

I tried Donna's office several times, but there was no answer. I needed some friendship, so I swung by Malley's bar, where he can usually be seen having a microwave sandwich for lunch, which is just what he was doing today.

He was also watching the noon news. "Reagan, man, he's made a big difference in this country."

"Yeah. Most of us are starving to death."

"Crap—he's the best thing that's happened to us."

"I'd hate to see the worst."

He glowered and went back to watching the tube. The local newsman was of the hair-spray, Ken doll type. With his big hairy paw, he gestured at the screen. "Lookit that bastard. So pretty." He minced his voice. "I seen this Sid

Caesar routine once. Had a guy like this newscaster, right? Only when the camera went around his back, there was this windup key. The guy was like a prop or something."

For some reason Malley's image made me laugh out loud. Maybe I needed relief from knowing that Jane Branigan was being booked, from knowing that my detective days seemed far behind me. Thus far I'd proven myself to be pretty inept.

"Good to hear you laugh," Malley said. "You had me worried the other night. You were really down."

I kept watching the screen. I suspected that there was indeed a windup key sticking out of the newsanchor's back.

"Now all I got to do is get you fixed up with the right broad," Malley said.

"I think I met her."

"What's her name?"

"Donna."

He thought about it. Apparently if her name had been Polly or Sheena, he would have complained.

"Not bad," he said. "College grad?"

"Yeah. Why?"

"You're making a mistake."

"Why?"

"When you think about it, we all had good mothers, right?"

"Right."

"And not one of them was a college grad."

"Yeah. I guess so."

"Well."

"Well, what?"

"So how come you're so unhappy with broads all the time?"

"Maybe because I'm a jerk. Maybe I make myself unhappy."

"Uh-uh. It's because you go out with college grads. I mean, look at the fucking record. Your wife was a college grad, right?"

"Right."

"Then Jane Branigan. College grad?"

I nodded.

"And now this Donna. Do I have to predict how it's going to end up?"

Malley always pursued his ideas with the passion, if not the panache, of an Oxford don in a debating society. He banged his fist and jabbed the air. He was a frustrated prosecuting attorney.

"So what'm I supposed to do, walk up to a woman on the street and ask her IQ?"

"Right," he said, "and if it's below sixty, jump 'er."

I didn't know which was funnier—his image of the windup newsman or his theory about the women in my life.

"Actually, I'd better go back and call her," I said.

"Cruisin' for a bruisin', Dwyer, that's you."

An Alabama song accompanied my phone call to Donna.

"I've been wondering about you," I said. "How's it going?"

Something was odd, wrong, in her voice. "Oh, pretty good."

"You sound really thrilled about hearing from me."

"Things are just a little screwed up, is all."

"Are you all right?"

"Oh, nothing's really wrong. Chad's just asked me to marry him."

I thought of Malley's theory. Maybe he was right. Maybe I should go out looking for a woman who liked "Gilligan's Island" reruns and thought Liberace was a concert pianist.

"You still there?" she said.

"Yeah." A frog the size of a Shetland pony had jumped down my throat.

"It's a bummer."

"There's an expression I haven't heard in fifteen years," I said. I tried to be light. Lead pancakes.

"I don't know what to do."

That line worked on me like surgery. Implicit in it was that she was at least thinking it over.

A familiar panic rose up in me, a mild form of hyperventilation. Damn, but I liked this woman and I didn't want to see her—

"How about going for a ride with me?" I said.

"Where?"

The idea was ridiculous and unnecessary and I knew she wouldn't go for it—but I also had the hope that she would say yes and be alone with me for a few hours and let my modest charms work on her.

"Tanrow."

"Where?"

"I told you. The other day. Those flowers being delivered."

"Oh. Yeah."

"There could be," I said, flinging my voice like a pair of doomed dice, "something important to the case there."

For the first time she sounded at least a tad less than suicidal.

"You really think so?"

"Yeah."

"You going now?"

"I thought I would."

I wanted her alone in my car.

"I don't know," she said.

"This could be the break we've been waiting for."

"Really?"

"Really."

"Well . . ."

"I'll be out in front of your office in twenty minutes."

I hung up before she could say no.

"I DON'T WANT TO LOSE YOUR FRIENDSHIP, no matter what happens," Donna Harris said when we were on the interstate and about ten miles from the exit that would take us to Tanrow.

A low sky filled with fat black clouds. Snow. Or rain. Or both. Lonely cows on frozen hills. Perfect complement to my mood.

During the drive she'd explained what had happened. How Chad had had some kind of "vision," it seemed. One that "proved" they were destined to be together. He was already in the process of dumping his stenographer. She was already seeing a Japanese shrink (the significance of his nationality eluded me, but I didn't say anything).

And so here was Donna, not knowing what to do. On the one hand she loved him ("I have to be honest with you, Dwyer"), but on the other hand she wasn't exactly certain about the quality of that love ("I've spent the last fifteen years of my life with him, maybe it's just a habit"), but then again there was me ("God, I really like you, Dwyer, I mean in all respects. You're really tender and you're really funny and you're really cute") and couldn't I see what a mess things were?

"But no matter what happens," she repeated, "I don't want to lose your friendship, all right?"

"Sure. We can always exchange recipes."

"I'm serious."

I went back to staring at the frozen farmland that cleaved the line of gray horizon.

I leaned forward and found a jazz station on the radio. Miles came on. Bleak as the day itself, but beautifully so.

"God, Dwyer, I hate to ask you, but could we change stations?"

"Why?"

"Jazz really bums me out."

"Jazz does?"

"That's why I listen to Top 40."

"Why?"

"It's just like Muzak."

She found a Top 40 station.

Despite her tear-threatening eyes and the sullen angle of her otherwise lovely mouth, her foot started tapping. I had to smile. She was crazy and I loved her. Maybe precisely because she *was* crazy.

"Maybe we should talk about the case," she said, seeing the Tanrow exit sign ahead.

"Yeah," I said, though obviously I didn't feel much like it.

"You think there's something funny about the flowers being delivered from here?"

"Sure." I explained about florists wiring or phoning orders to one another.

"So why didn't you just call the florist yourself?"

I decided to just admit it. "I wanted to be alone with you. Plead my case." I looked over at her. Held out my hand. She put hers in it. I felt wonderful and terrible at the same time—filled equally with hope and despair. "I don't want you to go back to your husband."

"I know you don't, Dwyer, and I'm sorry things are so screwed up."

146

I let her cry.

She leaned over and snapped off the Top 40. "That stuff's such shit," she sobbed.

Tanrow was one of those movie-set little towns you see less and less often in the Midwest these days. A town square complete with Civil War memorial and bandstand. Neat little businesses with striped tarp awnings built around the square. A church steeple like a rocket against the sky. Big-eyed children marking the progress of our car, our out-of-county license plates making us curiosities of a sort. A theater with a marquee at least forty years old sat on the corner where we pulled into a parking place. I could imagine the marquee resplendent with such names as Alan Ladd and Randolph Scott and Rory Calhoun.

The truck I'd seen the other day was parking in an alley next to the florist shop.

We sat staring at the place, the people going in and out. One of my bucolic moments overcame me. I'd always had this fantasy of moving to a small town such as this. Start another family. Learn how to talk to birds and plant tomatoes. It's never going to happen.

"Gee, this is the first time I've really felt like a detective," Donna said.

"Why?"

"I don't know. Just sitting here. Watching. Kind of a stakeout, right?"

"Yeah. I guess."

"I'm sorry things are so crazy, Dwyer."

"I know."

She touched my hand again. "You know I like you."
I nodded.

"Let's go," I said.

The various flower scents combined to create an almost narcotic odor, like a room where marijuana is smoked too much and too often. My stomach curdled.

"Boy, doesn't it smell beautiful in here?" Donna said.

On either side of the place were big refrigerated glass panels behind which lay jungles of flowers. A neat little man with horn-rimmed glasses in a white doctor's smock was making up a colorful arrangement. "Hi," he said in a booster-club voice, "may I help you?"

I put out my hand. He shook it with a hard, quick grip, like a snakebite. "Ab Windom," he introduced himself. Then I showed him my license."

He looked at me with a smile on his face. "I think we should give you some sort of plaque or something."

"How's that?"

"I'll bet you're the first private investigator who ever set foot in Tanrow. "You're about as unlikely as an astronaut coming through here."

"Well," I laughed, "it's nice to be a pioneer, I guess."

"How may I help you?"

"Your truck was in the city the other day." I gave him the Dodson woman's address.

"Sure," he said confidently. "We're there every week."

"Every week?"

"Yes, and have been for the past six years."

"Mind if I ask why?"

He smiled. "The customer wants it, that's why. Two dozen roses. Once a week."

"Why don't you just wire the flowers?"

"Like I said, that isn't what the customer wants."

"Would you tell me who the customer is?"

He shrugged. "To tell you the truth, I don't know."

"What?"

"Afraid I don't."

Donna looked at me and said. "Well, how does he get paid?"

"Ask him," I said.

She turned to Windom. She was nervous. "How do you get paid?"

"You must be his assistant, right?"

"I'm a reporter," she said. There was pride in her voice. Even confidence. It was fetching.

"Reporter? Hey, what's going on here?" He adjusted his glasses as if to get a better look at us.

"A murder investigation," I said, hoping the ominousness of my remark would ensure his cooperation.

"You're kidding!"

"Afraid not."

"God. A murder investigation."

"So how do you get paid?"

"Well, every month I get a money order."

"Return address?"

"Your hometown. Just the postmark."

"You say this has been going on for six years?"

"Yes. A man called me back there. Placed a standing order. I haven't heard from him since."

From my wallet I took a clip of the newspaper story concerning Stephen Elliot's death. "You ever see this man before?"

He stared at it and started to shake his head no, and then he said, "Why, my God, that's Gil."

"Gil?"

"Gil Powell. I wouldn't have recognized him."

"You know him?"

"Knew him. He grew up in Tanrow. Then he—Well, something happened." Windom seemed reluctant to talk. "Lot of painful memories for this town."

Donna said, "Like what?" She was getting better at it.

The door opened behind us. An elderly couple came in. Windom excused himself. The couple wanted an anniversary corsage. They were in their seventies and holding hands. I admired and envied them.

"Maybe we're on to something," Donna said excitedly.

"Maybe we are."

"God, this is great."

Then Windom came back and she was all business again.

"What about the painful memories?" Donna said.

Windom shrugged. "Well, it's no secret. He got himself involved—romantically involved, if you understand me—with a high-school teacher. The woman was a—well, very beautiful, very high-strung. There were some who said she was insane and some who said she was an alcoholic. But—" A kind of sadness came into his eyes. "I was single myself in those days. Had a few dates with her. She was very—sophisticated—for a town like Tanrow. Didn't have many friends. Then she and Gil—"

This time it was a young man who came in and interrupted us. He seemed as nervous about buying flowers as I'd been at his age buying condoms.

Then a middle-aged woman walked through the door.

Windom smiled. "Business is getting good. Tell you what, who you should talk to, I mean, is Mrs. Paul Rutledge. She had a rooming house where the teacher stayed. Mrs. Rutledge is in the phone book."

"Thanks," I said.

I turned and started to leave.

"Wait a minute," Donna said. "You forgot to ask him something."

"What?"

"Mr. Windom?"

"Yes," he said, turning back to Donna.

"What was the teacher's name?"

"Oh," he smiled. "I forgot to tell you, didn't I? It was Eve. Eve Evanier."

THE RUTLEDGE HOUSE WAS ONE OF THOSE big old three-story jobs that seemed ideal for hiding secrets. Shuttered windows hid the interior from scrutiny and the chipped paint and the leaning chimney spoke of tough times. A lean dog that seemed to be all ribs and teeth flung himself at the car like an arrow.

"No way," Donna said. "I'll wait here."

"Hey, detectives and mail carriers aren't supposed to care. We go anyway."

"Not me."

"C'mon."

I opened the door to show her that I wasn't afraid. Then the mutt tried to eat my hand. I closed the door instantly. His head came up to the window. He showed me his molars as if I were doing a dental inspection.

"God, look at him," she said as he drooled all over the window.

His spittle formed clammy puddles on the glass. He was pretty disgusting.

Donna and I sat back and watched the house. The only

thing that struck me as odd was the Oldsmobile convertible parked at an angle to the house. Ready for a fast getaway.

"How are we going to get in there?" Donna asked.

"Simple. I'm going to drive right up to the front door and we're going to make a run for the screened-in porch. We should be able to beat the dog."

"You're kidding."

"Nope."

"You're really crazy. He'll gnaw my leg off by the time I get to the porch."

"Lucky dog." Even given the turmoil of our emotional life, I had hardly forgotten how desirable she was. So far all we'd shared was some relatively chaste kissing.

I started the car again.

"You ready?" I asked.

"Jeez."

I put the car in gear. Drove up to the porch. My plan was simple. Run for the door. Fling it open. Keep the dog outside.

"Okay," I said.

And I took off.

The Rutledge house was located on the edge of town. There were no other houses within a half mile. The dog could eat us and nobody would know. He got close to my heel, but I did a kind of kick—part kung fu, part Fred Astaire—and held him off just enough so that I could reach the steps three feet away.

"Shit!" Donna screamed behind me.

She was only two steps behind me. "Hurry up!"

I reached the screen door, ripped it open, and let her run in past me. Then I jerked the door closed and watched the mutt hurl himself against the screening. He was mad.

Donna was ecstatic. "We showed *him*."

"Yeah. We did."

"He really pisses me off."

"The dog?" She sounded as if she were describing Richard Speck.

"Who else would I be talking about?"

"Oh."

The front door led to a venerable vestibule that smelled of old wood, dust, and furniture polish. A different world spun in the molecules of this place—the world of my grandfather. We went inside.

On the right wall were several handmade wooden mailboxes. They stood empty. I glanced inside. Dust had accumulated in them an inch thick. The rooming house had fallen on hard times long ago.

"Mrs. Rutledge?" I called out.

I looked up the winding staircase that disappeared above. No sign of anybody. Nor was there any in the corridor that led to the main part of the house on this floor.

In the lemony-smelling gloom, Donna leaned in and took my hand. "Kind of spooky."

"Yeah." I kept thinking about the woman Eve. I also kept thinking about the Oldsmobile parked at such an odd angle outside. "Let's try the parlor."

The hallway creaked as we walked. Donna kept glancing up at the ceiling, as if she expected us to be attacked by bats. By the time we reached the parlor the hallway had gotten almost dark.

From beyond the double sliding doors came the faint sound of a radio tuned to a station that still played Mantovani albums. I knocked. Once. Nothing. I tried again. The sound seemed brittle, almost vulnerable in the turn-of-the-century silence. Still nothing.

Donna screamed before I really saw anything. They came out of the gloom near the back. Two of them. Wearing masks.

Wouldn't you know—Frankenstein and Dracula.

They had been hiding in the deep day-end shadows collecting around a walk-in pantry.

They seemed to be wearing the same clothes they had worn the night they'd attacked me outside the bar. Now they'd added guns to their outfits.

"Get in there," Frankenstein said, waving his weapon.

"God," Donna whispered. "A criminal."

"Yeah," I said, "he probably has a record and everything."

"Shut up and get in there," Frankenstein repeated. His mask distorted the true quality of his voice.

I opened the sliding doors. There was a gray-haired woman in a faded housedress tied to a straight-backed chair in the middle of the room. She'd been gagged.

Dracula said, "We warned you, pal. The other night. Now it's too late."

"She'll choke to death," I said.

The way the woman swallowed, I could see she was having trouble breathing.

"Let me loosen her gag," I said.

"A fucking boy scout." Frankenstein laughed.

I went over to the woman. Took the gag off.

She had a fleshy, wrinkled face. Her eyes scanned me in gratitude and terror. "They wanted to know about Eve."

"Shut up," Frankenstein said.

The five of us said nothing for a time. I looked around the room. There was a mantel filled with black-and-white framed photographs. Shawls and doilies covered the armchairs and the lumpy couch. Ferns in various stages of dying stood in the northern-light window. The faint radio played Jo Stafford now. We were trapped in a time warp.

Dracula went over and got two more chairs. Donna glanced at me anxiously. I tried to calm her with my expression, but I was anything but calm myself.

Then it was our turn to sit down and be tied to the chairs. They made quick work of it, tying the knots tight enough to cut off the circulation in our wrists and ankles.

But they weren't through, of course. This was just the beginning.

Dracula went out of the room. You could hear the dog coming back into the house with him. The mutt's paws scratched on the hardwood floors as he slid around.

Then the animal shot through the doors and crouched in front of us, baring his teeth.

"We ain't through with the old lady," Dracula said.

"Come on, Samson," he said, snapping his fingers.

He brought the dog over to the old lady and said, apparently to me, "You interrupted us. We gotta finish our business."

In the dying light the two looked comic—and all the more ominous for the comic aspect—their masks cheap and gaudy and very unreal-looking.

The dog had no problem seeming real. His coat was shaggy and dirty and his breath was bad. His eyes were red, as if he had a hangover, and his snout was slick with snot.

Nothing about him suggested what came next. It happened so quickly I scarcely noticed.

The mutt banged his head against the old woman's leg and ripped a long, clean gash into the flesh.

The dog started barking and the woman started screaming.

Frankenstein came over and slapped her once, hard, across the mouth.

"Now, I want to know where the strongbox is that Eve gave you."

But Frankenstein had overplayed his hand. The woman was in such agony that she seemed not to hear him. She moaned, pitching from side to side inside the constraints of the rope.

Donna's eyes filled. I wanted to hold her. Reassure her. Hard to do with your arms cinched by rope.

"The strongbox," Frankenstein said again.

The mutt had moved back a few feet, waiting his call.

"I don't have it," the woman said miserably.

"Bitch," Dracula said.

He said "Beefsteak" and the dog lunged at the woman. This time he raked his teeth down her other leg. He had begun to smell. A kind of lust.

This time the woman put her head back and started to

shake it from side to side. I wondered how long Frankenstein and Dracula had been here. They seemed like patient boys. Maybe a long time.

We sat there twenty more minutes while it went on. The dog had a go at her three more times. The last time he got her hand. He was extremely well trained. He didn't make a mess. He just inflicted very precise pain, making holes in her skin, blue where puckered, red where the blood came slowly forth. The dog cleared up any doubts I'd had about Frankie and Drac. Not punks at all. Pros.

"Stop it!" Donna screamed at them toward the end.

But they were having too much fun with the old woman to pay any attention.

Then above all the noise—the dog growled steadily, like a beast in a slasher movie—and the two thugs kept up steady cursing beneath their masks—I heard the car.

As daylight waned in the parlor, tires crunched on gravel outside. I felt an idiotic relief. A movie formed in my head. The florist back in Tanrow hadn't trusted us and had sent the local cops to check us out. Here they were now. Boy, were these two bastards going to get theirs.

For what seemed an hour or two there was no further sound from outside.

Had I imagined the car crunching on gravel?

The dog went on snarling, hunching, ready for another lunge; Frankenstein and Dracula kept up their demands; the old woman said "I don't have it, I don't have it," in a kind of rosary of pain; and I let my mind wander to the strongbox and realized that it was probably the key to everything, from the murder of Stephen Elliot to the deaths of the motel clerk and the hooker.

Then I heard footsteps on the front porch and the rusty hinges of the door squeaking open.

The thugs heard the noises too.

They snapped a command to the mutt, "Ease, boy, ease." He went into a state of suspended animation. The one with the Dracula mask jerked a Luger from the belt inside his jacket and started toward the sliding doors. The other came over to us. We knew better than to talk.

"Shit, it's you," Dracula said in the hallway outside. "Scared the shit out of us."

Frankenstein waved his gun at us, glanced at the mutt crouching by us, then went out into the hallway too.

The shots came very quickly.

Four of them.

As abrupt and final as an execution.

Two bodies collided with the floor.

Donna looked over at me as the steps started toward us.

We were next. Or at least I thought we were, but then there was the sound of an oncoming car on the lonely road.

Steps retreated from the hallway. Down the front stairs. A car motor twisted to life. Tires on gravel. The whine of a transmission in reverse.

Gone.

"My God," Donna said. "My God."

There wasn't much else to say.

THE ONCOMING CAR BELONGED TO AB WIN-
dom, the florist. He came in, took a startled
look at our bonds, and proceeded to set us
free.

"Did you get a look at the car?" I asked.

"Afraid I didn't," he said. "I was listening to the Cash
Call Contest on the radio. I was pretty engrossed."

"Why'd you drive out here?"

He flushed. "Well, to be honest, I got to thinking that
maybe I shouldn't have trusted you as much as I did. No
offense. I just wanted to make sure everything was all
right."

Later, after we had rubbed some circulation back into our
arms and legs, this is the story Mrs. Rutledge told us.

In the early sixties a very beautiful but frail highschool
teacher named Eve Evanier came to Tanrow. The eligible
bachelors of the community were enchanted, if a little
frightened—her honey-blond hair, her curiously gentle
manner, her melancholy silences confused them. If she'd
been a carhop, they'd have had no problems with her. But,
given the fact that she was so shy, given the fact that she

never seemed to go anywhere but to work and church, they didn't know what to make of her.

The women of Tanrow did, of course. Eve Evanier's mailman told everybody that she received *The New Yorker* and *Evergreen Review* by subscription, which marked her as slightly sinister in the eyes of the women. Then a local sheriff's deputy named Sale told of stopping her one evening while she walked and finding her absolutely drunk. This was all the nervous men and the jealous women needed—some objective proof of her moral shortcomings. Now they snickered at her openly, and many housewives talked of going to the school board and getting her fired.

Which was when Eve and Gil Powell began spending time together.

Gil was, like the Evanier woman, an outcast. His father, a handyman, was long dead and his mother spent her nights dancing in the plastic glow of big Wurlitzer jukeboxes and sleeping with traveling salesmen. Gil possessed only one real virtue—his looks. It was widely said that he could go out to Hollywood and become a movie star. The problem was he had nothing to put with his looks—he wasn't intelligent or sensitive or funny. He was, in fact, more a mannequin than anything. He stayed by himself. You saw him most often watching TV and shooting baskets in his driveway. He was a terrible basketball player.

In his senior year Gil happened to take an English course taught by Eve Evanier. On the first test he got the lowest grade she'd ever given out to anybody not retarded. She called him into her office. That was the day it all started. Within a week Gil Powell drove his 1953 Chevrolet fastback out to Mrs. Rutledge's rooming house, where Eve stayed, nearly every night. Everybody knew what was going on. Gil seemed amused by the affair. Eve took it desperately seriously. Gil's mother called the Evanier woman several times, threatening her; she even sent a beefy used-car salesman named Dolan out there to call the Evanier woman a slut; but Gil and Eve Evanier became inseparable.

She was good for him. He'd been dull—now at least he made a pass at reading and developed something resembling a sense of humor. She bought him clothes and taught him how to dress. The snobby girls of his class, who'd always avoided him before, starting writing him notes and working him into their more lurid conversations.

Tanrow people often saw Gil and Eve in nearby towns—dancing very tightly in supper clubs to steamy records by Frank Sinatra and Tony Bennett. Once Gil and Eve were even seen checking into a motel. There seemed to be no end to the scandal. Gil was eighteen; Eve was thirty-six, a dipsomaniac old maid who'd taken up with a veritable kid.

Not that Tanrow permitted it to go on indefinitely. Three weeks before the end of Gil's senior year Eve Evanier was fired by the school board. The session was open to the public and the public turned out. Not even the annual Tanrow-Capitol City football game rivaled the attendance that night. Eve was flayed, flogged, and removed in scathing language, language she'd never forget.

So Eve Evanier left Tanrow with Gil in tow. Or the kid who used to be Gil, anyway. Now he was tall and trim and looked a great deal like Natalie Wood's husband, Robert Wagner. With Eve's help, he dressed a bit like him too.

Mrs. Rutledge, whose husband had been a drunk himself, a man given to not paying his bills and to making scenes with "respectable" folks, had become a friend of Eve's during all this. She liked the woman, felt sorry for her, feeling that Eve was in some way not quite right—not just alcoholic, but clinically ill in some other ways. She felt anxious for Eve too—the Evanier woman put everything she was and owned into Gil. Someday she would be old and no longer beautiful in her fragile way and Gil would leave her. Mrs. Rutledge feared for that a great deal.

So Eve and Gil left Tanrow and nobody, not even Mrs. Rutledge, heard from them for fifteen years.

Mrs. Rutledge began to wonder if Eve were even alive any longer.

160

But it wasn't, as things turned out, Eve who died. It was Gil Powell. Eve put the unsophisticated small-town boy to rest and resurrected him as somebody witty and elegant and polished as chrome—Stephen Elliot.

"The last couple of years, Eve started calling me again. Stopping out sometimes," she said. "That's why those men came here. They knew she started leaving things here."

"What things?"

She shrugged. "A couple of trunks and cardboard boxes of old junk. I'm not sure. I never looked through it."

"Why'd she leave it here?"

"She said somebody was trying to get it. She wasn't sure who." She sighed. "Then that guy was out here a couple of weeks ago."

"What guy?"

She described him.

"What did he want?"

"Oh, he didn't come right out and say what he wanted. Said he was running a credit check on Eve. But I wondered if he wasn't—what's the word?—you know, *casing* my place."

The same thought occurred to me. I'd even begun to suspect who'd hired Frankenstein and Dracula. And Mrs. Rutledge's description wasn't far off.

"When was the last time you spoke to Eve?"

The Rutledge woman frowned. "Week ago. But I didn't talk directly to her. She—she has these spells, kind of. Withdrawals. I talked to her man, Kenny. He said she wasn't doing real well. He was thinking of putting her in a hospital." She shook her head. "Mental hospital."

Donna looked at me. She was still frightened from the gunshots. She just stared. All Ab Windom could seem to do was shake his head.

"My God, I don't want to see what's out in the hallway," Mrs. Rutledge said.

Donna grabbed my arm as we left the parlor.

Only police photographs do justice to murders. The blood

is usually sloppy, as if it had been sprayed over things, and even black-and-white snaps capture the peculiar colors of dead skin. The two thugs' eyes bulged at nothing. Frankie's shirt was soppy with leakage from his stomach. Drac had been caught in the throat. His twisted fingers gave the impression he'd been clawing at something. Behind us the mutt growled. I snapped out the command phrase: "Ease, boy." He obeyed.

"God," Donna said, "there are flies and bugs."

As, indeed, there were. Already. Crawling on the dead bodies. It's sort of a quick reminder of the messiness of existence, the flies and bugs.

I helped her find the bathroom. She wanted to be sick alone.

When Ab Windom helped Mrs. Rutledge pack—he was going to take her to the doctor and then to a nearby town where she could stay with a cousin, her tolerance for excitement having been passed a few weeks before—Donna and I went upstairs to look at the things Eve had stored.

Past a painted-over door, in a room thick with dust, was a lifetime collected in four cardboard boxes and a steamer trunk. Letters, faded photographs, souvenir menus, and maps and pennants described the past twenty-five years of Eve Evanier's life as busy but curiously hollow. Especially when you read some of the letters Stephen Elliot had written her.

"He really was scum," Donna said.

From the tone of most of the letters it was obvious he knew that Eve Evanier was mentally ill—probably hopelessly schizophrenic. He was polite enough to her, but there was a placating tone to the words—as if he were addressing someone he was impatient with.

Then Donna found a stash of Eve's letters. They were straight out of Tennessee Williams. Florid, overwrought, sad. They described a woman who had made her young protégé the center of her life. For a time the protégé had responded appropriately. They'd lived together as lovers. But you could see that he had begun to withdraw, to find other interests.

"God, I really feel sorry for her," Donna said.

"Yeah."

Then she smiled, tapping a stack of letters Elliot had written to Eve. "He must've gotten a lot better at writing at some point too. His letters are nearly illiterate."

I smiled back. "Professional jealousy?"

"No. He's really bad."

I went through the remaining boxes of memories. All lives could be reduced to this. Mine would be someday. My son would look at odds and ends—cuff links and an appliance store receipt and maybe a slightly out-of-focus photo of me at the beach or in my cop uniform—and that would be the only proof he would have that I'd ever existed at all.

When I finished I turned around and found Donna staring out the window at the dusk.

"You okay?"

"Maybe I'm not cut out for this, Dwyer. There are two dead bodies downstairs. There's a really depressing story in all these boxes. And it doesn't seem to bother you. You just go right on with your work."

"Maybe that's how I deal with it."

"Shit, I don't know," she said.

I went over and knelt down next to her. I put my arm around her and lost my face in her hair. I'd forgotten about Donna's impending decision. About Chad's marriage offer. Now it came back to me. Chad was probably offering her a slightly better life than any I'd come up with. "Maybe I should just get another agency job," she said.

I stood up. "I'm going to call the sheriff. Explain what happened," I said. "Then we'll go back to the city. I need to look somebody up."

"Who?"

"The guy who came out here a few weeks ago pretending to run a credit check."

Interest stirred in her gaze. "You know who it is?"

"Maybe."

"Who?"

"When I know for sure I'll tell you."

"Thanks a lot. I thought we were working on this together."

It was easy to see I had made her mad, but before I could say anything she stomped out of the room, having to duck her considerable lovely height to pass beneath the frame.

31

"I'M SORRY I WAS SUCH A JERK BACK THERE," I said as we took the exit ramp into the city. The sheriff had come and we'd answered his questions. The ambulance had taken away Frankie and Drac—who, without their masks, had been just as unknown to me as before—and Ab took Mrs. Rutledge to the doctor.

The forty-mile trip back had been made in silence. Every time my jazz song ended she punched into Top 40. Every time her song ended I punched back to Jazz. This was how, as far as I knew, most mature and responsible adults behaved.

"You really were a jerk."

"Thank you," I said.

"You're welcome."

Silence again as the neon glowed in the harsh cold night. An early Christmas tree had appeared on top of an appliance store. The decorations, given my mood, seemed almost obscene.

"You're taking me home?"

"Yes," I said.

"And where are you going?"

"I'm not sure."

"I'll bet I know."

"Where?"

"To the guy who went out to see Mrs. Rutledge."

"I guess that has crossed my mind."

"You bastard."

"I just didn't think you'd be in the mood. After the bodies this afternoon—"

"Get something straight, Dwyer. Just because I get depressed once in a while doesn't mean I don't come from very strong stock."

"Right."

"What is 'right' supposed to mean?"

"Just that you're sounding tired and cranky and a tad hysterical."

"You don't sound so hot yourself, you asshole."

"Well, does that mean you want to go with me then?"

"You're darn right it does."

I pulled into a drive-up phone to get his address from a directory. He lived where the rest of the extremely successful yuppies did, in the rambling hills ringing the east side of the city. The section had become a hymn to redwood and the great god Porsche.

His address gave me an idea. I called the guy from my security agency who'd run a credit check on several people for me. My man sounded as if he'd been asleep for the past four hours. He tried to sound happy to hear from me. He wasn't especially convincing.

"Didn't turn up a hell of a lot that was especially interesting."

I mentioned the name of the man I was about to see.

"He was the only one with any promise."

Then he checked off some extremely interesting stats. I thanked him, promised him a steak dinner, and hung up.

"We may have our man," I said.

"Well, I suppose now you're going to tell me. Right?"

"David Baxter."

"You're kidding."

"Uh-uh, the guy at my agency tells me he's way

overextended, a prime candidate to be a blackmailer. He's desperate for money."

Fog moved across the streets in the hills like something alive. The interior of the car still echoed with our exhaustion and shot nerves and misplaced anger. I put a hand over and held it there and finally she took it, but without any enthusiasm. I withdrew it. Then a few minutes later she put out a hand. I didn't have much enthusiasm for her gesture either. She sighed and shoved both her hands into her pockets.

Through the shifting white moisture you could glimpse expensive homes of the modern variety, mostly variations on the ranch style, which clung to the contours of steep hills. Country-style mailboxes announced the names of owners. I drove past the one we were looking for, then had to back up to find it.

Before I whipped up into the drive, I said, "I'm tired of fucking arguing."

"So am I."

"I'm sorry you had to see the bodies this afternoon."

"So am I."

"Maybe you're right. Maybe you're better off going back to an agency."

"I'm really thinking about it."

"I don't blame you."

I really didn't.

The drive, narrow, steep, was like shooting up a tunnel. I used the fog lights to get me even with a picket fence and then I stopped the car.

I opened the door, started out. Then I looked back at her.

"You all right?" I asked.

"Yes," she said.

But I knew better. Her hands were shaking and her eyes were dead and glazed and without their remarkable luster.

"I've never seen anything like that before, Dwyer." I could tell she wanted to cry. I wished she could.

This time when I held out my hand she took it and held it very, very tightly.

"Would you mind if I just sat here?" she asked.

"Of course not. I just need to ask him a few questions."

"You really think he did it?"

"I'm not sure."

"Oh, Dwyer." Then the tears burst. "Just get out of here, would you?" she said.

I looked at her, realizing with a terrible force that I loved her.

I closed the door.

My shoes in the damp grass sounded the way they had the day I'd met Jane Branigan in the park—sucking up the moisture of the ground. Through the fog I saw a light burning in the front of the house. I squished across the lawn and reached the porch and rang the bell. The chimes were absurdly loud and happy-sounding in this twilight zone.

Nothing.

I clanged the chimes again.

An owl answered, a throaty, eerie, pulsing noise against the night.

It took minutes for me to hear it, and at first I couldn't identify it. Then the sound began to assume a shape for my mind to perceive—like a form gathering substance, approaching out of the fog.

A woman moaned.

I thought of Donna in the car. But she was too far away. I moved carefully, like a blind man, closer to the picture window. I put my ear to the cold glass. The moaning came from inside. I put my arms out stick straight and walked carefully toward the door. I didn't want to trip on anything and knock myself out.

The knob would not turn.

I felt through the murk and found that the upper half of the door was glass. I took off my jacket and slammed my fist into the smooth surface. The glass shattered. No problem then to reach inside and turn the knob.

The house smelled of whiskey and cigarettes. In the corner of the living room a small night-light burned. The room was modern and severe and harsh.

The footsteps came from the back of the house—steps slapping against tile. A door slammed. Then I heard the steps on the damp lawn outside.

I ran to the back of the house to see if I could catch the owner of the footsteps. But in the kitchen, in a pool of blood even worse than the one Frankie and Drac had lain in, were the Baxters.

They had been shot several times in the face and chest. Their killer must have had to reload at least once.

The smell, the high, iron, rank smell of fresh blood, made me nauseous. Blood had sprayed against the white stove and the yellow dishwasher. Shining liquid dollops of it shimmered in the dim illumination from the porch light out back.

Incredibly, then, Lucy Baxter's arm moved. Just a twitch. But I saw it and knelt down.

My first thought was to see if I could give her CPR.

She reached up and grabbed me by the lapel with startling strength.

"She's got it," she said.

She was a caricture of a good-looking woman. But now her features were exaggerated. The blood, thick and slow in the corner of her mouth, drooled across my hand.

"I don't understand," I said. "Who's got what?"

"Eve," she said. "Eve's got it."

I realized there was time only for a few questions. I gently put her back down, stuffing my jacket under her for a pillow. I got up and soaked a dishrag in cool water and started to clean her face.

She floated in and out of consciousness. A part of me watched her die, fascinated, curious about what she was experiencing. Was she seeing a white light? Hearing angels sing? Or only sensing a vast, waiting nothingness?

She came up out of her death long enough to grab my hand once again as I daubed at her face with the dishrag.

"I'm really scared."

I held her hand. "Your husband killed Elliot, didn't he?"

"No."

169

"There's no point in lying now, Lucy."

"I'm—not—lying."

"But he was blackmailing everybody—"

"Yes—blackmail—but— He—killed—David—the—others—"

A terrible revelation came over me. I'd assumed the man we were looking for was David Baxter because of his financial problems. But now—"

I started to ask her another question, but she tugged on my hand again.

"I need to say a prayer," she said. Then, "Touch my stomach."

"What?"

"Please. Touch my stomach."

I put my hand down there. He had shot her just below the sternum. There was a hole you could drop fifty-cent pieces into. I wanted to hold her back from death, like tug-of-war, but I knew it would be no use. The coldness from the other side started to chill me too.

I touched her stomach, the burgeoning roundness of it.

She started to cry.

"I finally get pregnant, we waited so long, I finally get pregnant and look what happens."

The refrigerator started to thrum and the dishwater cranked into a new cycle.

There amid all the electrical appliances, she died. She and her baby.

I stopped only long enough to call Edelman and tell him where to meet me.

Then I ran from the house, suspecting I was already too late, dreading that the footsteps I'd heard running out the back door of the Baxter place had already claimed their next victim.

There was only a piece of her torn coat lying on the seat when I flung the car door open.

He had taken her.

THE POLICE HAD CORNERED OFF THE DEAD-
end street where Eve Evanier lived under
the name of Helen Dodson.

Neighbors were out in pajamas and robes, pointing to the
Dodson house through the fog, as if a Japanese movie
monster were about to come looming up out of the
darkness.

I got out of the car so quickly I banged my knee. I
hobbled over to the nearest policeman and showed him my
license. He waved me through. Edelman was waiting for
me.

Two steps across the threshold, I thought of the Rutledge
woman's parlor. Despite the modern house outside, the
interior here was an anachronism. The furniture was bulky,
and sculpted walnut. Doilies were on every available
surface. Floor lamps with intricately patterned shades threw
soft shadows against the wall.

In front of a fireplace, sitting primly on a divan, was a
beautiful, white-haired woman. It was impossible to guess
how lovely she'd been earlier in life.

Next to her was a tall, severe man dressed in livery. It
was a three-piece suit, but it was also the uniform elected by

some domestics. He held a hypodermic needle up to the firelight and squeezed a drop or two of liquid out.

Edelman stood watching him. When he saw me he put a finger up to his lips and nodded to the man.

"Just relax, Eve," the man said.

She hadn't noticed me before. She looked up, smiled. In her high, old-fashioned lace collar she might have been posing for a cameo brooch. "Why, aren't you Stephen's friend?" she said to me.

Embarrassed, I moved my head in a way she apparently took to be a nod.

"Did you bring him home with you? He's always staying out late. Then he has to get on my good side by getting me the penthouse at the hotel." She laughed with a lover's secret enjoyment.

She sounded friendly and happy. Then the needle was pushed into her arm.

I watched her features look—just for that moment of pain—their real age there in the firelight and the decades-old glow of this museumlike room.

But I couldn't wait any longer. I crossed to Edelman. "Have you seen him?"

He shook his head. "Her man there, Farrady, says he was here earlier tonight. He had a gun and he got what he came for." Edelman nodded to Eve Evanier. "Farrady had to give her a sedative. She's got a heart condition. Apparently she hasn't been able to deal with Elliot's death at all, and Farrady's afraid she's going to die."

I grabbed him. "You coming with me?"

"Where?"

"There's only one place left to look. Come on."

You might imagine that riding beneath a siren gives you a lot of power. It doesn't. It just makes you a potential victim. Many people, you see, don't move over to the curb for you. They try to beat you or race you. Or they've got their stereos up so loud they don't even hear you.

I hadn't been in a patrol car in several years. I rode shotgun while Edelman drove. The siren sprayed blood into the night—it was a day and night filled with blood—first the thugs—then the Baxters.

By now what had happened and who the killer was no longer mattered. Now I had to find Donna. I tried not to think of what might have happened to her, what, in his psychosis, he might have done to her.

"You sonofabitch," Edelman said.

"What?" I said, coming out of my reverie.

"Not you. That motherfucker in the middle of the intersection. Won't move."

So we went around him. Dangerously. Just like in the movies. Only Edelman was no stunt driver, believe me. And I was no stunt passenger.

The parking lot held two cars when we got there. A garbage truck was eating a dumpster.

The elevator took us swiftly and silently up seventeen floors. Edelman had his piece out. It shone with oil. It was ready. So, apparently, was Edelman. "You like her, huh?" he said, trying to cool me down.

"Yeah."

"Well, hell, good for you."

"I hope she's not dead." I was starting to lose it.

He threw an arm around me.

"Trust your Uncle Edelman, okay rookie?"

"Yeah."

"And blow your fucking nose."

When the elevator doors opened I recalled the night when I'd come up here with the porno photos and met Phil Davies. And the absolute sense I'd had that somebody was watching me from the shadows.

I put a hand out, stopping Edelman.

"What?" he said in his normal voice.

"Sssh."

Both of us peered into the darkness.

I heard her before I saw her. A moan somewhere in the gloom.

I froze. Sweat bloomed on me. Edelman put an avuncular hand on my arm. I let him lead the way over to her.

It wasn't Donna. It was Carla Travers. Or what was passing for her these days. Moonlight sliced by the blinds fell across her tubular body as she tried to crawl away from us. She was no trouble to stop. Edelman just walked around her and stood with his long legs together. She looked up and moaned again, a fat, soon-to-be-old lady with her media-rep hair sprayed hard as a helmet and a sick gleam in her eye.

Edelman reached down and helped her up. He didn't bother to hide his distaste. There was no time for pleasantries. That was the first good look I got at her bruised and cut face and the wristbone that jutted through her flesh like a piece of decorative glass. Apparently he'd beaten her for quite a while. This kind of punishment took time.

A few moments later my eyes dropped to the square metal box she'd crawled away from. The strongbox so many people had been looking for. That so many people had died for.

I bent down and picked it up. I walked a few steps closer to the blinds, where the moonlight waited.

The whole thing had been alphabetized. Sometimes there were photographs, sometimes there were note cards. I went to the Ts, pulled Carla's. The notation was surprisingly formal: "Carla Travers is receiving kickbacks from two ad agencies with whom she's working a con regarding billing." Then there were two additional names, presumably the agency people Carla worked the scam with.

The rest of the contents of the strongbox was like that. Names, dates, notations. There was some ballpoint writing on the back of Lucy Baxter's nude photo with Davies. It read "The faithful Mrs. B." I didn't feel like looking any longer.

I glanced over to see Edelman holding Carla while she vomited into a wastebasket.

I reached them just in time to hear a few more strangled splashings. Edelman made a face. Then he took handcuffs from his belt and clamped her to a chair.

The noise in the night startled the three of us. Big speakers woofy with the sounds of commercials. The screening room. Bryce Hammond was back there.

We moved through the shadows toward the noise. Edelman's Smith and Wesson glinted occasionally with the mercury-vapor light spilling in from outside. The air was rife with the smells of furniture wax and coffee.

"What the fuck's he doing?" Edelman whispered, nodding toward the screening room.

"Jacking off."

"What?"

"Playing his frigging commercials."

"I thought Elliot was supposed to be the genius up here."

"That's what Bryce Hammond wanted you to think."

"You're gonna have to explain that to me." He waved his piece. "Some other time, though, okay?"

We reached the screening room. He stood on one side of the door. I stood on the other.

He said, "Hammond, make it easy on all of us. Just put down your weapon and come out."

A minute later Edelman said, "Did you hear me, Hammond?"

No response either time.

Only the loud bright noise of award-winning commercials.

In the shadows I saw Edelman's large Adam's apple bobble up and down. He shot me a bemused expression and then we both lunged.

The noise of the large wooden doors being thrown back was drowned out by the commercials. We went in.

She sat on a chair on one side of the console that controlled the big videotape machine.

At first paralysis overcame me. I thought she was dead.

But then my eyes fell to the steady rhythm of her breathing and I relaxed.

I started to look to Edelman, but at that moment the bullet came from nowhere, crashing through the din of the soundtrack, and Edelman spun around. His gun went off, but only into the ceiling. He glanced at me—a plea of fear and terror—and then collapsed in two jerky, seriocomic movements.

And then he appeared.

He wore his commodore's outfit and a kind of sad smirk, as if he knew the joke, this time, was on him.

He carried a Luger, the drama of the weapon fitting his style.

He came up from the shadows in the corners of the large room, stepping over Edelman's fallen body and moving toward me.

Instead of speaking to me directly, he nodded to the screen. Looked lovingly on his work up there—a woman whistling while she did her gardening.

"You figured it out, didn't you, Dwyer?" he said.

"No, actually Donna and a bartender named Malley did. Or at least they gave me the clues. Malley told me about a comedy skit where a man was nothing more than a windup toy—just the way Stephen Elliot was for you. Then Donna pointed out that when you looked at something Elliot actually wrote, he was nearly illiterate."

As I spoke, I looked over nervously at Donna. I assumed she'd been knocked out and would survive. But now, since she had yet to move, I had begun to wonder.

Another commercial came on. A hamburger that had little tap-dancing feet and did a version of "Yankee Doodle Dandy."

He went over and sat down on the chair next to Donna. He picked up a martini glass. It was full. Apparently he'd been drinking from it before.

I looked over at Edelman. He'd been my friend. Some terrible weariness pushed through me, blocking out even anger. The way he'd fallen, his arm seemed to have broken. His weapon was inches from his fingers.

Hammond said, "I became passé. I was a product that no longer sold. So I invented a new product. Stephen Elliot. I told him all the right things to say, all the right things to do, all the right places to go—and I, secretly, did all the work." He shook his handsome white head. Bitterly. "Clients just automatically assume you burn out when you reach your forties. So I created Stephen Elliot."

"He wasn't the blackmailer, Hammond. Baxter was."

He smiled sadly. "I know that now. Stephen didn't have to die, after all. Just David."

"Just David and Lucy and the motel clerk and Jackie-the-hooker and the two punks in the Frankenstein and Dracula masks."

He looked surprised at my tone of indignation. "As far as I'm concerned, that blood's on Baxter's hands, not mine. He forced me to do what I did." He set his drink down. "Believe it or not, Dwyer, I'm a man of principle. I was just trying to stop people like Phil Davies from being black-mailed." He then spent the next four wobbly minutes wearily reciting what had happened, how he'd found out about the whole blackmail scheme when Davies's behavior toward him started to change—his old friend and client had now become an enemy of sorts and, when he asked Davies what was wrong, Davies told him. Hammond then started to follow Elliot around, which was how he learned about the motel clerk and the hooker, Jackie, who helped set up others of Hammond's clients for blackmail photos. By then he was crazy enough to kill everybody involved—it had become a kind of crusade—and he would have murdered Donna, Mrs. Rutledge, and me, too, this afternoon, if the florist hadn't come along.

"The irony, of course," he went on, "was that not until yesterday did I find out that Baxter was the really vicious one in this whole thing." He paused, glancing at Donna, then up at me. "Elliot liked the pictures because they gave him certain kinky kicks, but Baxter was making a lot of money on what was in the strongbox, really bleeding people." He shook his head.

He put the Luger closer to Donna's head. "The people I've had to deal with . . ." He laughed bitterly. "Carla Travers. That scummy motel clerk. Those two thugs I hired to help find the strongbox and to keep you off my tracks. And Elliot—" He shook his head again. "Elliot wanted to prove to Baxter that he was in control after their partnership began. So he got Lucy Baxter to pose with Davies. She was so much in love with Elliot that . . . Elliot took that picture himself. Jane was in love with him, too, as you well know. I almost did her a favor when I found her in Elliot's apartment and put the gun in her hand. She was really insane at that point, strung out on alcohol and drugs. She came in and passed out right away. That's when I put the gun in her hand. I took her over to the body so that when she woke up she'd think. . . ."

Hammond seemed much older now. Exhausted. "He needed money, Baxter did, that's why the blackmail thing appealed to him."

Hammond picked his drink up again. "Poor Eve—that's how I met Stephen. She brought him up here, years ago, to apply for a sales job. Came right along with him. As if she were his mother." He finished his martini. He took the glass in his palm and smashed it hard against the console. Blood ran down his fingers instantly. The pain seemed to give him some satisfaction. "Everybody died so fucking unhappily. Only Eve was spared the sorrow—crazy as a fucking bedbug. Probably always has been." He was doing *King Lear*. Raving. He threw his hand majestically to the screen. "Those are all the things that made Stephen Elliot so famous. But I wrote them. Every last fucking one of them. And I made him rich too."

For the past few minutes I'd been watching what was about to happen peripherally. All I would have time to do was dive for Donna and knock her out of the line of fire.

"The only reason I killed them, Dwyer, was to protect my clients, I swear to you," Bryce Hammond said. "I swear to you. He blackmailed them all."

Edelman got up on one knee.

I put my head down and dove for her.

Hammond saw what was going to happen. He brought up his Luger.

Edelman opened fire.

The gun roared above the soundtrack. Like God's wrath finally manifest.

After several long minutes I got up. I didn't look at what was left of Hammond. There'd been enough death impressed on my vision.

I just grabbed Donna and pulled her up against me tight and struggled my way out of the screening room that had been Bryce Hammond's temple.

33 I WISH I COULD TELL YOU THAT A LOT OF really dramatic things happened as a result of Bryce Hammond's death. But not much did, really. Donna, Edelman and I went to the nearest emergency room. Edelman was worked on and went home. Donna, who'd only been knocked out, was checked for a concussion, then left on the arm of Chad, whom she'd called soon after reaching the hospital. I ended up spending the hours till dawn talking to a detective named Sullivan, patiently explaining the case and all its entanglements.

Carla Travers, who in addition to having a wrist fractured in three places also had a concussion and two broken ribs, had told Edelman and me everything from her hospital bed.

The time I'd visited her apartment and heard her say, "You know what I want and I better goddamn get it," she'd been talking to Baxter. She wanted money, or she threatened to expose the entire blackmail scheme to the police. But then she got a better idea—she would find the strongbox herself and begin her own blackmail plan. She had used Elliot's alcoholism against him but was now playing against somebody treacherous—Bryce Hammond.

The watching eyes I'd felt on me that first night I'd been

at Hammond's agency had belonged to Carla. She'd been there to steal the box, thinking Elliot might have hidden it in a trick magic box he'd been given by Eve as a present— Elliot being the kind of drinker who talked too much, eventually told his sycophant Carla nearly everything. But Carla hadn't found the box. So that night at the hotel she joined all the others in the room to demand that Baxter stop blackmailing them, Baxter being the culprit that Stephen Elliot had named to her. Only not even Baxter had the box that night. It then resided at Eve's, where Elliot had hidden it before he died. Bryce Hammond had exhausted all other possibilities but Eve's—where he went and found the strongbox.

Of course, Carla had mistakenly blamed Eve for everything all along, anyway. Elliot's whining, drunken conversations had led her to believe that Eve had hired the thugs who broke into Carla's apartment—when it had been Bryce who'd hired them to search for the strongbox.

Carla related all this in a voice she'd borrowed from a corpse.

Then I went out and had a huge breakfast and woke up late the next morning to a ringing phone to find that I'd been selected to play the daddy in the pizza commercial, after all. In the afternoon I visited Jane Branigan and her parents in the hospital. It was a melancholy hour.

That night I went to work. The old bastard who always tries to steal ham came in and tried again. This time, being broke, I just scooted him out of the store. After my shift was over I went to Malley's, where he told me about this really stupid woman he thought I should date.

Then I went home and that's where I saw her. Sitting in my parking lot. The way she'd been the first time I'd seen her. She rolled down her window.

"You want to get in and smoke?" she said.

"I don't know."

She smiled. "You playing hard to get, Dwyer?"

I shrugged. "Maybe I'm just tired."

"You should read the story I wrote for the first issue of *Ad World*. You come off sounding like Dashiell Hammett."

I just stared at her. "I missed you."

She took a while to say it. "I missed you too."

"What about Chad?"

"Honest?"

"Honest."

"I don't know."

"I'd be a lot better for you."

"I think you would be. At least, sometimes I think you would be. I'm pretty confused, Dwyer, about a lot of things. All the killings—you and me—"

After awhile I said, "Maybe I can help unconfuse you."

"Maybe you can."

"If I get in, can we listen to a jazz station?"

She laughed. "You're crazy, you know that?"

I got in and shut the door and immediately pulled her to me. "Look who's talking," I said.

About the Author

Edward Gorman is himself an advertising executive, living in Cedar Rapids, Iowa. He is the author of one previous mystery, *Rough Cut*.

Attention Mystery and Suspense Fans

Do you want to complete your collection of mystery and suspense stories by some of your favorite authors? John D. MacDonald, Helen MacInnes, Dick Francis, Amanda Cross, Ruth Rendell, Alistar MacLean, Erle Stanley Gardner, Cornell Woolrich, among many others, are included in Ballantine/Fawcett's new Mystery Brochure.

For your FREE Mystery Brochure, fill in the coupon below and mail it to: